Heart
2 HEART

What Reviewers Say About BOLD STROKES Authors

DIANE AND JACOB ANDERSON-MINSHALL
"With its expected unexpected twists, vivid characters and healthy dose of humor, *Blind Curves* is a very fun read that will keep you guessing." – *Bay Windows*

ANDREWS & AUSTIN
"In a succinct film style narrative, with scenes that move, a character-driven plot, and crisp dialogue worthy of a screenplay, Andrews & Austin have successfully crafted an engaging Hollywood mystery… series." – *Midwest Book Review*

KIM BALDWIN
"*Force of Nature* is filled with nonstop, fast paced action. Tornadoes, raging fire blazes, heroic and daring rescues…Baldwin does a fine job of describing the fast-paced scenes and inspiring the reader to keep on turning the pages." – *L-word.com Literature*

ROSE BEECHAM
"…her characters seem fully capable of walking away from the particulars of whodunit and engaging the reader in other aspects of their lives." – *Lambda Book Report*

GEORGIA BEERS
"Beers weaves a tale of yearning, love, lust, and conflict resolution. She has constructed a believable plot, with strong characters in a charming setting." – *JustAboutWrite*

RONICA BLACK
"*Wild Abandon* tells how these two women come to realize that 'life was too precious to be ruled by…fears, by…demons.' While these two women struggle with their issues, there is some very, very hot sex. If you enjoy complex characters and passionate sex scenes, you'll love *Wild Abandon*." – *MegaScene*

GUN BROOKE
"*Course of Action* is a romance…populated with a host of captivating and amiable characters. The glimpses into the lifestyles of the rich and beautiful people are rather like guilty pleasures…a most satisfying and entertaining reading experience." – *Midwest Book Review*

CATE CULPEPPER

"…an exceptional storyteller who has taken on a very difficult subject …and turned it into a spellbinding novel. As an author, she understands well that fiction can teach us our own history." – *JustAboutWrite*

JANE FLETCHER

"*The Exile and the Sorcerer* is a mesmerizing read, a tour-de-force packed with adventure, ordeals, complex twists and turns, and the internal introspection of appealing characters." – *Midwest Book Review*

CATHERINE FRIEND

"Friend tackles both science fiction and romance in this adventurous tale... A most entertaining read, with a sequel already in the works. Hot, hot, hot!" – *Minnesota Literature*

JENNIFER FULTON

"A deliciously sexy thriller…*Dark Valentine* is funny, scary, and very realistic. The story is tightly written and keeps the reader gripped to the exciting end." – *JustAbout Write*

JD GLASS

"*Punk Like Me*…is different. It is engaging. It is life-affirming. Frankly, it is genius. This is a rare book in that it has a soul; one that is laid bare for all to see." – *JustAboutWrite*

GRACE LENNOX

"*Chance* is refreshing…Every nuance is powerful and succinct. *Chance* is not a novel about the music industry; it is about a woman discovering herself as she muddles through all the trappings of fame." – *Midwest Book Review*

LEE LYNCH

"Lynch, with a dozen novels to her credit dating back to the early days of Naiad Press, has earned her stripes as a writerly elder.She was contributing stories to the lesbian magazine *The Ladder* four decades ago. But this latest is sublimely in tune with the times." – *Q-Syndicate*

JLEE MEYER

"*Forever Found*…neatly combines hot sex scenes, humor, engaging characters, and an exciting story." – *MegaScene*

Visit us at www.boldstrokesbooks.com

Heart
2 HEART

by

Julie Cannon

2007

HEART 2 HEART
© 2007 BY JULIE CANNON. ALL RIGHTS RESERVED.

ISBN10: 1-60282-000-7
ISBN13: 978-1-60282-000-5

THIS TRADE PAPERBACK IS PUBLISHED BY
BOLD STROKES BOOKS, INC.
NEW YORK, USA

FIRST EDITION, DECEMBER 2007

CREDITS
EDITORS: JENNIFER KNIGHT AND J. B. GREYSTONE
PRODUCTION DESIGN: J. B. GREYSTONE
COVER GRAPHIC: SHERI (graphicartist2020@hotmail.com)

By the Author

Come and Get Me

Acknowledgments

To all the wonderful women at BSB, thank you. Again, two simple words don't seem enough to possibly convey my message, but everyone who has been through this process knows what I mean. Jennifer—thanks for being the master editor. Sheri—thanks for taking my crude concept and making it fabulous. JBG—thanks for crossing the *t*'s and dotting the *i*'s. And thanks, Rad, for having faith in me.

According to the Organ Procurement Transplant Network, there are over 100,000 people in the United States waiting for an organ transplant. Each year hundreds die while waiting for the *Gift of Life*.

DEDICATION

To my Mom, who talks with pride about her
daughter, the executive, globe-trotting,
lesbian-romance author,
and not necessarily in that order.

To my family, who are as proud of me and my
success as an author as I hoped they would be.

#1—you continue to be all that, and then some.
I'm so very proud of you.

To Alex and Emily. Sorry, there are no pictures in
this book that Mommy wrote either.

And finally to my best girl Laura.
From my Heart 2 your Heart.
I love you.

CHAPTER ONE

H ello stranger. Where've you been?"
Lane almost dropped the plate of muffins she was carrying. The husky question had come from a table behind her. Butterflies crowded her stomach as she turned to face its occupant, a tall, lean woman with dark brown hair, eyes as green as a summer field, and a genuine smile that completely lit up her face. "Detective Bain, hello."

Kyle stood up so fast she had to steady her chair to prevent it from toppling. "Do you have a minute to join me? I haven't seen you in ages."

"Of course, you're one of my favorite customers." Lane's eyes quickly swept over the woman she had not seen in months.

The detective was never other than immaculately dressed, and today was no exception. Her trousers held a crease that would cut butter, and her starched blue linen shirt only attempted to disguise the strong muscles underneath. When the weather was cool, she typically wore a matching blazer, but today she sat uncloaked, displaying the weapon on her hip and the gold shield on her belt.

Kyle laughed. "You really should raise your standards." She held Lane's chair as she sat down. "How are you? I heard you were ill."

"Just a pesky virus that took a little more out of me than I expected, but I'm better than ever now." Lane didn't want people to fuss over her or treat her any differently just because she'd been seriously ill. She was the same person she'd always been, with the exception that she now treasured each day she was alive.

"You look great." Kyle couldn't help but move her eyes over the slim body in front of her as if to verify her first impression.

Lane Connor was just as beautiful as ever. Her blond hair was a shade lighter than Kyle remembered and was secured by a bright green ribbon. Her white tank top contrasted with tanned shoulders and firmly developed biceps. She crossed legs that were equally tanned and showed the evidence of hours spent running on the beach. Kyle's fingers tingled with the desire to run her hands over the smooth skin. She tried to drag her eyes away from temptation but instead took another languishing look over Lane's body. When she paused at the radiant face, Lane's twinkling blue eyes told her she'd been caught looking.

Feeling self-conscious, Kyle sat down and picked up her coffee mug to mask her tongue-tied nervousness. As she sipped, she watched Lane swat away an annoying fly. The movement called attention to her left hand, which showed no sign of the ring worn so prominently the last time Kyle saw her.

Lane caught the change in expression as Kyle studied her hand. The detective wasn't the first person to notice the absence of her ring, and the unfamiliar butterflies in her stomach fluttered again. "Thanks, I'm feeling better every day."

It was the truth and just the day before, Lane's cardiologist had given her a conditional bill of good health. Of course the conditions were that she had someone else's heart beating in her chest and she would have to take anti-rejection drugs for the rest of her life. But if she took care of herself, she would have the same life expectancy of any other woman currently in her mid-thirties.

"The body's resilience is amazing." Kyle wanted to kick

herself as soon as she delivered this benign pronouncement. Finally, an opportunity to say something personal and that was the best she could do?

She was surprised at how rattled she felt seeing Lane again. It had been over a year since their last conversation, and theirs was no more than a passing acquaintanceship. Kyle was still a beat cop when she'd first noticed Lane several years ago. She would stop and chat when she saw her. At first she was just doing her job, establishing relationships with the people on her beat, but after awhile she simply liked talking with Lane. Of course, an added plus was that Lane was usually in a pair of shorts, t-shirt, and work boots. Kyle admired the fact that she took a hands-on approach to refurbishing the old building that had become the restaurant she was sitting in now. When The SandPiper had finally opened for business, Kyle was one of the first customers, and she'd continued to stop in a few mornings a month.

She typically sat on the patio quietly enjoying the morning sun and the antics of the people as they walked, ran, and skated by on the boardwalk in front of her. The crashing waves of the Pacific Ocean were strangely comforting as they glistened in the early morning hours. The air was crisp and clear, punctured with the staccato sounds of seagulls searching for breakfast. Early on she had admitted to herself that she didn't frequent the restaurant for its scenic views. She always hoped to catch a glimpse of the owner and better yet, share a cup of coffee.

Kyle had always found Lane attractive, but the two carat diamond ring she wore screamed "off limits," and over time they had shared polite casual conversation with neither of them stepping over the unspoken boundaries. Kyle had been extremely worried when she learned that Lane had been ill, but it was really none of her business. She didn't realize how much she'd missed her until she saw her again after so long.

"You're right about the resilience," Lane said with a hint of irony. "I got sick, almost died, and my girlfriend left me, all in the same week. And here I am, I think the better for it." She watched the detective's reaction closely.

Kyle felt as if her world had tilted. *Lane could have died? And her girlfriend had dumped her? Jesus H. Christ.* In the twelve years she had been on the La Jolla Police Department, Detective First Grade Kyle Bain had learned to temper her expressive eyes. It was imperative to the success of her work as a homicide investigator that the criminals she interrogated could not read her facial expressions. However, this was a totally different situation, and she didn't even try to guard her reaction.

"Makes my broken water pipe seem a little trivial," she replied flippantly. Cops were famous for their gallows humor, a natural defensive mechanism to maintain their sanity when faced with the ugly horrors of life. Kyle was suddenly afraid she had treated Lane's situation too lightly.

"You certainly know how to put things in perspective, Detective."

"Occupational hazard." Kyle was relieved when Lane laughed. Her smile lit up her face and made her eyes crinkle.

A loud banging sound on the boardwalk drew their attention. A man lay slumped at the base of a light pole, a large metal trash can rolling on the sidewalk beside him. Blood seeped out of a cut on the left side of his face. Kyle suspected he had collided with the pole and that the reason for his distraction was walking toward them now.

Lane watched as Kyle's attention was drawn to a blonde on rollerblades. Her extremely large breasts bounced beneath less material than a cocktail napkin.

"Ouch, poor guy. I wonder how he's going to explain the stitches." Kyle remarked wryly. A cut that bled like that would need to be surgically closed.

"Something other than the truth, I suspect." Lane's eyes were on the woman skating by. "No wonder he crashed. No one has breasts that perfect."

Did she just say what I thought she did? This was new, Kyle noted. During their many conversations Lane had never alluded to anything sexual. Their conversations stayed on safe topics. A chuckle escaped Kyle's lips.

"Not without several thousand dollars and a good plastic surgeon."

Lane suddenly wondered what Kyle would think about the average size of her breasts. Or would the nine inch scar snaking down the center of her chest be her point of focus. A knot gripped her stomach at the thought. It was a fear that had started to creep into her consciousness lately. Before her illness, Lane was in top physical condition. She was a triathlete, competing in several Ironman competitions a year. Training made her muscles firm and her skin tan, and she was one of those rare people who didn't have a freckle or blemish anywhere on her body. She had worked hard in the past few months to be able to regain her stamina to work every day. And even though she could finally run several miles on the beach without gasping for air, the ugly scar would always remind her that she would never be the same person she was a year ago.

"You don't approve of breast enhancement?"

Holy shit. What's going on here? Kyle had an odd sense that she was somehow putting her foot in it, but she wasn't sure how. She had never understood why some women felt the need to have breasts larger than life. She enjoyed breasts as much as the next lesbian, but her level of arousal certainly didn't go higher in proportion to her partner's cup size. She tried to read Lane's face before answering, but the woman would have made a good detective. Her expression gave nothing away.

"It's not for me to approve or disapprove." She looked directly into Lane's eyes. "I prefer women who are confident enough with themselves as they are, flaws and all. None of us are perfect, far from it."

Lane held the direct gaze for a moment. "You've got a point. However, there are times when surgery is the only solution to fix something that has gone terribly wrong." She left her comment hanging in the air waiting for Kyle's response.

"That's true, but I don't think that not being happy with the size of your breasts is 'something that has gone terribly wrong.'" Kyle stopped when she realized how harsh she sounded. She smiled. "I guess I might be a bit more judgmental than I thought I was."

Lane's pulse raced faster when Kyle laughed. "That's okay. It's those little faults that make us cute."

Kyle swallowed hard, her skin burning as if Lane could see through her clothes.

Lane watched the pulse in Kyle's neck quicken. She waited a minute before she stood.

Kyle stood as well and held her chair out. Lane stepped the closest she had ever been to the woman and said quietly as she walked away, "Keep the streets safe, Detective."

Kyle had to lean forward to hear the parting words, and when she did, she smelled a combination of perfume, sun, and sea air. The odor was intoxicating. Her head spinning, she sat down and stared at the crashing waves. *What in the fuck just happened?*

❖

Lane's phone was ringing when she stepped into her office. It was her private line and when she answered, she was greeted by her brother's cheery voice. John lived in Hong Kong and had taken the first flight to Los Angeles when Lane became ill. He had stayed in town until the doctors were certain she was out of danger and had then returned to his wife and children. For the first few weeks after her release from the hospital he'd called every day. Once it became apparent that Lane was recovering, they'd allowed the calls to dwindle to one or two a month, so she welcomed the chance to catch up and exchange family gossip.

As her brother talked, Lane's mind drifted to her conversation with Kyle Bain. Kyle was always confident and self assured, but she had appeared to be at a loss for words more than once this morning. Lane was intrigued to realize that every time their eyes met, she felt a connection she'd never been aware of before. It wasn't unusual for her to experience a sense of pride when a customer returned, and she'd particularly enjoyed the detective's company. But the flicker of awareness between them was completely new.

Lane had always thought Kyle was attractive, and occasionally she'd had the impression that Kyle was interested in her, but she'd never responded or even mildly flirted; she had a partner after all. After eight years together, she and Maria had been living what she thought was a good life. Their house was within walking distance of the beach, they had good friends, and the restaurant was turning a profit.

Lane drew a slow, controlled breath at the thought. Her illness had taught her many things, one of which was that she refused to dwell on shit she had no control over. Life was too short. Like her diseased heart, Maria was a thing of the past, and Lane wasn't sure who had suffered more pain over the whole fiasco, she or her brother.

John had broken the news to her three days after her surgery, that Maria had packed up and moved out. After she had been blatantly absent from Lane's bedside, he had gone to their home looking for her and it was quickly apparent that she was gone. Lane had been hurt and angry, but she knew even then that if she wanted to live, she could not let the shock of Maria's abandonment influence her recovery in the slightest.

"Lane, are you even listening to me?"

The sound of her name jolted Lane back to the present. "Of course I am," she lied.

"Then why have I repeated the same question three times and you still haven't answered me?"

Lane knew her brother wasn't mad at her, but she apologized anyway. "I'm sorry John, my mind was on a customer I had this morning."

"Trouble?"

Lane smiled at her brother's concern. Even though he was several thousand miles away, he would come to her rescue in a heartbeat if he thought there was a problem. "No, on the contrary, it was very nice. Someone I hadn't seen since before I got sick." That was what she called her brush with death—getting sick.

"Do I detect something in your voice?"

"No, John you don't."

"Lane, are you starting to go out?"

"We've already talked about this." Several times as a matter of fact. John had been pestering her to start dating for the past few months.

"And you told me to mind my own business and believe me, I'm trying. But you're my baby sister and I love you. I want you to be happy."

"I am happy John. I'm alive."

"Lane, being happy is more than just being alive. Even for someone who went through what you did."

Lane leaned back in her chair. "I love you too. If it weren't for you I don't know how I would have gotten through all this. But I *am* taking care of myself and when I'm ready to start seeing someone, you'll be the first to know."

"Okay, okay, I'll step back…at least for a little while."

They chatted for a few more minutes before Lane sent her best wishes to his family and dumped the phone back in its cradle.

Despite her intentions to get some work done, her thoughts strayed relentlessly to Kyle. *Why did I flirt with her like that?* Word had spread quickly that Lane was single, and she had a never ending stream of invitations. Some were just looks from across the room, some were subtle inquiries and some were downright blatant offers to fuck. She had gone out a few times during the past few months, but none of the women sparked the kind of interest she seemed to have in Kyle all of a sudden. *Good god, I don't even know if she's involved with anyone!* Prior to her illness, Lane had suspected that Kyle was single, but a lot can happen in a year. *Boy, is that an understatement.* Lane felt almost giddy thinking about it. How could such a feeling spring from nowhere?

❖

Kyle was greeted at the door with wet, sloppy kisses. "How's my little sunshine today?"

She picked up the squirming toddler into her arms and closed the door behind her. She couldn't image her life without this enthusiastic greeting. Hollie was the spitting image of her mother, which made her the spitting image of Kyle, her mother's twin. Anyone who saw them together would never think that Hollie was Kyle's niece, but rather her daughter.

Kyle was determined that Hollie would know everything

about the wonderful woman who had died giving her life.

Sometimes when she looked at her niece the terrible days of the past year felt like just yesterday. She had eagerly anticipated the birth of Alison's first child and was thrilled when her sister asked her to be in the delivery room. The man Alison had been seeing for several years had no interest in fatherhood and had not returned any of her calls since she informed him of the baby. Alison had been crushed but refused to force him into something he clearly didn't want. She went as far as to serve him with paternity papers which he promptly signed relinquishing his parental rights. All that ugliness aside, Alison's pregnancy was a joyous time, one that had changed Kyle's life in more ways than one.

For Kyle, the most wonderful sound in the world is the sound of a newborn baby crying, and that's exactly the way Hollie Elizabeth Bain entered the world. Kyle had never seen a baby so small, and when the nurse handed the squirming bundle to her, she heard Alison laugh.

"She won't break Kyle."

"I know, but she's so tiny I'm afraid she'll slip through my hands." She held the baby close to Alison who placed a sweet kiss on her cheek. Tears welled up in Kyle's eyes at the joy she felt for her sister.

A quivering hand reached out and stroked the baby's soft cheek. "Hello Hollie. I'm your mom." An instant later, all hell broke loose.

After a battery of tests the neurologist confirmed that Alison was brain dead. Three days later the tests were repeated, as required by law, and she was declared dead. The rest was a blur, but there was one day Kyle would never forget.

The pain was unbearable. If not for the innocent, living creature wrapped tightly in her arms Kyle would not have cared that she was alive. As she looked through tear-streaked eyes at the neatly arranged flowers on top of Alison's casket, she'd thought it ironic that something so beautiful was being used to hide something as terrible as what lay beneath it. The ceremony, pomp, and fragrant beauty could not hide the cold hard fact that the most important person in her life was lying dead in the casket in front of her.

She'd kissed Hollie's head. *Oh, Allie. How will we ever go on without you?*

But somehow they had. One day at a time for Hollie and one minute at a time for Kyle. She was named Hollie's legal guardian and had subsequently adopted her niece. The days immediately following Alison's funeral were filled with diapers, formula, and sleepless nights, and Kyle had found a sense of comfort with the infant. The pain of losing her sister was still with her, but Kyle was finally at the point where thinking about Alison did not bring her instantly to tears.

"She was a joy as usual." Hollie's nanny, Gretchen came to the door wiping her hands on a dish towel. "We went to the park and she loved going high on the swing."

"That's my little daredevil. Big girls aren't afraid to go high are we?" Kyle was rewarded with another sloppy kiss.

"Well, dinner for Mommy is in the oven. You two girls have a good night. See you in the morning."

Kyle said good night to Gretchen and carried Hollie into the kitchen. Gretchen had come highly recommended from the nanny agency, and she and Kyle had hit it off immediately. Kyle had bought a larger house that included a separate guest cottage that was ideal for Gretchen to live in. The arrangement worked perfectly, and knowing that she could count on Gretchen when she was called out to investigate a homicide in the middle of the night allowed Kyle peace of mind.

She finally sat down several hours later, after bathing Hollie, singing her favorite lullaby, and tucking her in for the night. Much to Kyle's relief, Hollie had been sleeping through the night since she was two months old. When she first brought Hollie home, her mother and father had stayed with her for several weeks to help her adapt to being a new mother. They'd shopped for any of the necessary baby things Alison had not already purchased, and within days the spare bedroom was filled with brightly colored toys and every piece of furniture a new baby would need, including the crib that Hollie now slept in. When Gretchen arrived, Kyle had returned to work and her parents went home.

Hollie was an easy going thirteen-month-old but was shy around people she didn't know. It usually took quite some time for her to warm up to strangers, and even longer before she would allow them to pick her up. Kyle hoped that this cautious nature would continue through her childhood. She prayed every night that she had it in her power to keep Alison's daughter safe.

Since Hollie's arrival Kyle's social life had gone from active to none. Yet Kyle found she didn't miss dating and outings with friends as much as she'd expected she would. To her surprise, she looked forward to coming home after work and spending her evenings playing peek-a-boo and changing poopie diapers. She had remained dedicated to her job, but had gained an entirely new perspective on what was important in life. There was no disputing the fact that Hollie was her first priority.

Kyle stretched out her long legs and a stuffed Big Bird doll fell to the floor as she put her feet on the coffee table in front of her. She sipped a cup of tea that had been hot and steaming twenty minutes ago. The TV was on but she wasn't paying attention to the basketball players running back and forth across the screen. Her encounter with Lane Connor earlier in the day had lingered in her mind ever since, and now that she could finally relax, her thoughts drifted once more to the attractive restaurant owner.

Kyle didn't know if she'd been more surprised to see her back at work or to realize Lane had so blatantly flirted with her. Kyle was practiced in the art of sidestepping women who came on to her during the course of her duties, but she was flatfooted when it came to Lane—definitely out of practice. She hadn't gone out on a date or even spoken to a woman on a personal level since Hollie arrived more than a year ago. Even now, she was only barely able to make sense of what happened with Lane.

Kyle tried not to read more into their conversation this morning than what was there. She had an analytical mind and methodically weighed each piece of evidence in the cases she investigated. That knack carried over into her personal life as well. As she relived every word Lane said and evaluated the accompanying body language, she began to tingle. Lane's eyes had sparkled when they looked at her, and she had looked at her that way…a lot. She was definitely interested. Kyle leaned her head back on the couch and frowned.

Hollie was the number one priority in her life, and she could not imagine that ever changing. She had a responsibility to Alison and Hollie, and she was not going to let either one of them down. Her job was demanding, and there was simply no place in her life for a relationship. Maybe when Hollie was older, when she didn't need her as much, Kyle could reconsider. But when would that be? When she got into school? Then it would be homework and after school activities. Maybe when she was in high school and a little more independent? Kyle wasn't so sure about that, either. She'd seen the effects of parental neglect during this crucial stage of development and vowed always to be there for Hollie. Kyle groaned when she counted the number of years till college. She'd

CHAPTER TWO

K yle gathered up her keys and opened the front door, wiping oatmeal off her cheek at the same time. "Holy shit Travis! You scared the crap out of me." Her heart pounded at the unexpected sight of the man standing on her front porch.

Detective Travis Miller was thirty-two and often mistaken for a young George Clooney. He was happily married to his high school sweetheart and had a picture of his twin boys prominently displayed on his desk. When they became partners two years ago, Kyle did not disclose her sexual preference, which, like race, had absolutely no bearing on her ability to solve homicides. However, Travis was as good a detective as Kyle, and after several months he'd asked her point blank if she was a lesbian. Kyle had been hesitant to divulge details of her personal life, but Travis's gentle and understanding eyes were the mirror to his soul. She'd answered him truthfully, and they'd never looked back.

"What in the hell are you doing here?" she asked.

"Good morning to you too." Travis wiped something from her chin. "You missed a spot. I remember one time I had baby barf down the back of my jacket, and no one said anything until two o'clock in the afternoon."

"Thanks. I know you stopped by this morning for something other than to ensure my personal hygiene was up to par."

They both laughed and walked down the sidewalk to their cars.

"I'm coming with you for coffee," Travis said.

Kyle leaned against her car. "You're what?" she asked.

"I'm coming with you for coffee," he repeated as if she hadn't heard him the first time.

"You don't drink coffee, Travis."

Kyle had her suspicions about where this conversation was going. Travis was probably her best friend, and as best friends do, they could practically read each other's minds. It warmed her heart to know he was always looking out for her, but he had seemed way too interested in her love life when they were having lunch the previous day. She supposed she should have known better than to relay the details of her interaction with Lane, but she loved Travis like a brother and trusted him to keep the juiciest details to himself. He and his family had become an extended family for Hollie and they often babysat. Kyle returned the favor when Travis and Joann needed a night out without the clamoring of two six-year-olds.

"Ah yes, but you do, and you've developed a habit of drinking it at a quaint little restaurant that just so happens to have knock-out scenery."

Kyle folded her arms across her chest. "Okay, what's the deal Miller? I don't need a babysitter."

He smiled. "No, but you may need Cyrano."

Kyle was lost. "Cyrano?"

"Cyrano De Bergerac. You're obviously interested in Lane, and you may need some help asking her out, so I thought I'd come along and give you a hand."

He seemed so proud of himself, Kyle felt almost guilty about rejecting the offer. "I'm perfectly capable of knowing what to do with my hands." When a red flush of embarrassment materialized on her partner's face, she relented, Travis only wanted her to be happy. "Okay, Cyrano, lets go. But for the record, I'm not in the market for a relationship."

"Uh huh."

Kyle didn't need to look to know her partner had rolled his eyes at her declaration.

❖

Lane was anxious as she moved around the dining room checking on her morning guests. Her gaze kept straying to the patio in anticipation of seeing Kyle Bain again. During her morning run her thoughts had been filled with the charming, dark-haired detective. She had never looked at another woman while she and Maria were together. She was continuously on the receiving end of flirtations, but she never once gave them a second thought and certainly not in a sexual way. Until yesterday, when she saw Kyle again after so long.

Lane didn't remember consciously flirting with her, but when she replayed their conversation she realized she'd been slightly provocative. Judging by Kyle's reaction, the verbal banter was unexpected, and Lane wondered if she would be in for coffee this morning. She didn't know Kyle very well, but she was certain it would take a lot more than a few words to scare her off. Her heart skipped a beat when Kyle finally stepped out onto the patio. A split second later, her stomach dropped when she saw that Kyle was accompanied by an extremely handsome man who'd never been in The SandPiper before. They made a striking couple, and several sets of eyes were upon them as they walked through the room. Lane debated whether or not to visit their table, but before she could make up her mind, her legs started moving.

"Coffee for two this morning?" Lane asked. She knew Kyle was a creature of habit when it came to her morning coffee, at least what she ordered at The SandPiper. It was always simply black and hot. Lane had tried on many occasions to entice her to try something more interesting but so far had been unsuccessful.

As Lane approached their table, Kyle's blood pressure skyrocketed. Her smooth movement reminded Kyle of a silk scarf falling over bare shoulders. She hoped her voice wouldn't betray her racing pulse. "No, just one. Travis isn't a coffee drinker. Lane Connor, Travis Miller," she said by way of introduction.

Travis rose and extended his hand. "It's a pleasure to meet you. Kyle has told me so much about you."

I've what!

Lane was surprised. *She has?*

Nailed by a scathing look from Kyle, Travis tried to fake innocence. "What?"

Kyle sighed. "Don't mind him, Lane, he's just a dumb cop pretending to be a detective." She sent him a look that said: *Don't you dare open your mouth in front of her again.*

Lane quickly regained her balance. "I'm afraid you're one up on me, Detective. Kyle hasn't said a word about you." She looked at Kyle to judge her reaction to her statement and particularly the use of her name. Lane had always referred to Kyle as "officer" or "detective," never using her first name even though she knew what it was. She liked the sound of it, and if Kyle's reaction was any indication, she did as well.

Kyle's face softened. *She called me Kyle. God that sounded good.* "It pretty obvious why I like to keep Travis on a short leash. His mouth gets away from him sometimes."

"I'm also pretty good at reading people." Travis interjected.

Shut up Travis.

"Really? Do tell." Lane enjoyed watching Kyle squirm in anticipation of what her partner might say next.

Travis cast a mischievous look at the woman sitting to his left. "Considering my day-to-day happiness, and occasionally my life, depends on this woman," he tipped his head in Kyle's direction, "I'll pass on answering that and just ask for some hot tea."

Lane knew he was teasing Kyle and played along. She looked at Kyle but addressed her comments to her partner. "Be sure to leave me your card Detective Miller. We'll talk later." An air horn off in the distance brought her attention back from drowning in the dark green eyes locked with hers. She hesitated a second before addressing Kyle by her first name again.

"What would you like this morning, Kyle?"

Kyle dropped her head in her hand. *I'm going to die. Right here and now, I am going to die. No, worse yet, I won't.* "I think I need something stronger than coffee this morning."

"Are you interested in something hot or cold?" For a moment Lane was concerned about outing Kyle in front of her partner, but it was obvious from the look of enjoyment on Travis's face that her sexual preference was no secret.

Lane's voice was deep and husky and drew Kyle's attention back to her face. To the casual observer, Lane's expression was pleasant but her eyes housed a flame burning brightly. *Jesus.* Kyle summoned her dignity. "Surprise me." *I hope I can handle it.*

Well, well, well Detective. I see you do have an adventurous streak. "I know just the thing. I'll be right back." Lane kept her eyes focused on Kyle's for several moments and then turned and walked toward the kitchen.

"Jesus Christ Bain! I need to call the fire department to hose you two off."

Kyle let her gaze follow Lane's tight jeans-clad butt. "Go ahead, Miller, and when you're done I can use it to rinse out your mouth. What in the hell was that all about? 'She's told me so much about you.'" Kyle mimicked his previous statement. Travis placed his napkin in his lap.

"Well, you have."

"But that doesn't mean you have to tell her. Good God, Travis!" Kyle felt like she was in the middle of her adolescent years again.

"Look, I'm just some straight white guy, but if she came on to me like she just came on to you, I'd be all over her like white on rice. Why do the girls get all the *hot* girls?"

"I'll tell Joann you asked that." Travis loved his wife more than anything, and Kyle often thought that if she were straight, she'd want a guy like him. She was saved from his retort when Lane reappeared with their beverages.

"Here you are Detective Miller, one hot tea." Lane placed the cup and tea pot on the table in front of Travis. "And Kyle, something I made special just for you." Lane stepped around the back of Kyle's chair to serve Kyle from the right. She lightly ran her hand across Kyle's shoulders before she placed the glass in front of her.

Kyle's heart stopped when Lane's breast lightly brushed her arm. The clatter of the ice in the glass was an indication that Lane had felt the connection as well, and her hand shook as she set the drink down. Kyle swallowed hard when she envisioned Lane's hands on her body trembling with desire. It had been over a year since the last time she had anyone's hands on her body other than her own.

"Thank you," she managed to croak out.

Travis spoke up. "Can you join us for a minute?."

Lane looked to Kyle. "I won't be disturbing you?" *You'll definitely be disturbing me.* "I mean if you were going to talk about cop stuff?"

Travis answered before Kyle had a chance. "We don't talk about cop stuff before breakfast. Please sit down."

Kyle pulled it together enough to stand and hold the chair as Lane sat to her left. Her action was not missed by her partner.

"Are you going to eat that or can I have it?" Travis asked reaching across the table, his fork leading the way to the fluffy mound of whipped cream.

"You get any closer and you'll draw back a nub." Kyle teased her partner. She didn't know what Lane had brought her, but it smelled wonderful and she absolutely loved whipped cream.

"Aren't you going to try it and tell me what you think?" Lane asked nodding toward the glass sitting in front of Kyle.

The double entendre hung in the air, and Kyle answered the challenge with a tentative sip. She licked the residual traces of the white cream from her lips and placed the glass back on the table. "Just as I suspected. The perfect combination of sweet and spicy all in one taste."

"I'm glad you like it. It's raspberry-mocha frappuccino. You'll have to ask for it the next time you come in." *Okay, I'm getting in deep here, and if that didn't make my interest clear then I'll have to spill it on you next time.*

"I'll do that." Kyle let her gaze travel quickly over Lane's body as she sipped. She couldn't quite believe the stunning woman was flirting with her. She feared this was just a dream, and when she woke Lane would be gone.

New customers arrived, and Kyle lingered over her frappuccino so she could watch Lane smile, and walk, and angle her head the way she did when she took breakfast orders. Occasionally Lane glanced her way and made eye contact. Each time she did, Kyle's heart jumped so hard she almost gasped out loud.

"You done?" Travis asked with a quizzical grin.

Not even close. "Sure." Kyle dropped some cash on the table and stood. With a parting nod in Lane's direction, she left the restaurant with Travis and they walked through the parking lot toward their cars

"Jesus H. Christ, Bain! I don't know about you, but I need to go home and take a cold shower," her partner remarked.

I need more than a cold shower!

When she didn't reply he kept talking. "Holy shit, she's hot."

"Shut up Travis."

"What's wrong? I'm telling you she is H-O-T."

Kyle held her control by a thread. "I said shut up Travis. Your mouth is running faster than your hormones." Kyle unlocked her car door. Travis started to say something else and she quickly shut him down with a menacing, "Travis…"

"I know, I know, you're not in the market for a relationship. You know, you could probably use a good f—" He stopped in mid-sentence, realizing he'd gone far enough.

She knew he was a smart guy when he said he'd follow her to the station.

❖

The day dragged by, and it seemed like forever before Kyle was back in her car after the end of her shift. The pink message slip the station operator had handed her after lunch lay quietly in her lap giving no indication of the turmoil it caused her. Thankfully Travis was pre-occupied with dramas of his own and didn't see her step falter when she read the simple message: *I'd like to speak with you. Lane Connor.*

Kyle's hands were sweating as she pulled into the parking lot of The SandPiper. She had imagined several different scenarios for why Lane wanted to talk to her, but as she approached the front door, she had no more of a clue than when she got behind the wheel.

The interior was quiet without the morning hustle and bustle of silverware clinking on dishes bearing bacon and eggs. The aroma of coffee still permeated the air, and light jazz music was playing soft and low. Kyle had never been in The SandPiper at this time of the day, and she liked the quiet coziness. She looked around, not quite sure what she was doing here, when a soft velvety voice drifted over her shoulder.

"Detective?"

Her heart jumped for joy in hearing the familiar voice behind her. Kyle turned to face the woman she was there to see. "Hi," she said almost shyly. "I got your message."

"I'm sorry." Lane apologized. "I didn't mean you had to come here."

Kyle knew she didn't, but she wanted to see Lane again, if not to make sure she wasn't a dream then because she had missed her. "I know, it's on my way home, so I just thought I'd take a chance you were still here."

"Thanks for coming." Lane was suddenly tongue-tied.

"Is this an official visit?" *Please say yes.* Kyle's eyes were fixed on blue ones the color of the morning sky.

"No." Lane answered simply.

Oh shit.

Lane was concerned at the expression on Kyle's face. She expected her to turn and run any moment. "Would you like to sit down? You don't look well."

Kyle cursed her loss of control. As soon as she read the message, she knew this was a social call. She should have been better prepared.

"I'm fine. Really," Kyle added seeing the disbelief in Lane's eyes.

Lane searched the face in front of her looking for confirmation. "Will you have dinner with me?"

Kyle's heart skipped a beat. This was what she was afraid of. She wanted to have dinner with Lane and, if she were honest with herself, she was interested in more than that. But she had Hollie to think about. Either by design or sheer avoidance, Kyle had not yet found herself in this position. She wanted to say yes and she had to say no.

"I'd love to." She was immediately overwhelmed by guilt. *So much for parental responsibility.*

"Saturday night?"

Kyle's mind raced for an excuse, but she knew there was none. She would do dinner and nothing else. "Saturday's perfect."

Lane's smile lit up her face and her eyes sparkled.

"Seven o'clock? Do you like steak? We could go to The Stockyards."

"That'll be fine." Kyle was bumped by a customer coming into the darkened room, making her move closer to Lane than she'd ever been.

Their breasts brushed and Kyle's nipples tensed. Uncharacteristically unnerved, she shuffled her feet and put her hands in her pockets instead of where they wanted to be, untying the ribbon that held Lane's hair. Lane reached for a business card and pen lying on the hostess podium. Her hand shook slightly as she handed them to Kyle.

"Your address?"

"Right." Kyle chuckled, breaking some of the tension between them. "Look, can I meet you at the restaurant? My pager might go off, so I…" She let the comment die.

It wasn't a lie, her pager might go off but it would in all likelihood be Gretchen with some problem with Hollie. And Kyle didn't want to bring Hollie into the picture, at least not right now. Kyle was very protective of her daughter, and she swore that if and when she resumed dating, women would not be parading in and out of Hollie's life. Kyle wanted to get to know the woman before she introduced her little girl into the mix.

Lane frowned slightly in puzzlement. She wondered if she'd read too much into Kyle's responses when they flirted. She didn't seem especially eager to have dinner, in fact Lane had the impression she was looking for a way out. She decided to offer one but didn't get the chance.

Kyle forced a smile. "I'm sorry, I've gotta run. See you Saturday."

"I'm looking forward to it," Lane said.

All she got as Kyle strode off was a distracted smile and a mumbled, "Me too."

CHAPTER THREE

Lane finished examining herself in the mirror and buttoned the blouse that effectively hid the ugly reminder on her chest. The scar was becoming less and less noticeable as the months passed, but it seemed like only yesterday that she was sitting on a paper sheet in a paper gown in an examination room far too cold for her state of undress.

"Jesus Christ, Evelyn," she'd complained. "It's colder than a witch's tit in here. How do you expect your patients to get well if they're freezing their nipples off?"

"It's good to see you too, Lane." Dr. Evelyn Harris was a new, upstart physician when Lane came to see her for the first time seventeen years earlier. Over time, she'd administered antibiotics, antihistamines, stitches and an occasional cast for Lane and claimed she was her favorite patient.

"Other than bitching about my utilities, what brings you in today?" Evelyn reviewed Lane's symptoms collected by her nurse but preferred to hear it from her patients themselves.

"Cutting right to the chase today I see. What's got your goat?" This ritual bantering was a standard practice between them, and they enjoyed pushing each other's buttons to see who broke first.

"Nothing that a good romp in the sack won't cure. But that discussion is for another time. What's up? You look terrible."

"And I'm paying you how much for that official diagnosis?"

Evelyn grasped Lane's wrist and felt her pulse as she placed the stethoscope in her ears. Her face was a picture of concentration.

Lane sighed and leaned back on her hands. "I feel crummy Evelyn. I have no energy, a cough that won't go away and the chills. At first I thought it was a cold or allergies but I just can't shake it."

Evelyn launched into a series of questions about Lane's activities leading up to the onset of her symptoms. Forty five minutes and one complete physical later Lane was dressed and awaiting a verdict.

"They'll read your chest x-ray today and the blood work should come back in a day or two and we'll know more then. Your lungs sound a little scratchy and this script for an inhaler should clear that up. You probably caught a bug that's enjoying you as its host too much to leave." Evelyn winked at her. "Either way, I want you to pump up on the multi-vitamins and take it easy for a few days until we know exactly what's going on."

Lane felt no better after a few days, and several weeks later she'd collapsed at The SandPiper and was taken to the hospital by ambulance. She had been subjected to a battery of tests and could have sworn they'd taken half of her blood by the time Evelyn entered her room with a somber expression.

"Good God, Evelyn you look like you're about to tell me I'm dying." Her stomach plummeted when there was no smile in response to her joke. "Evelyn?"

"We've finally found out why you're not getting better. It's called endocarditis. That's an inflammation of the inside lining of the heart chambers and the heart valves."

"Okay." Lane had been sick before, and a shot or some pills

always took care of it. She had no reason to believe that would not be the case now.

Evelyn seemed to pick up on Lane's cavalier attitude, and her face grew sad. "No, Lane, it's not okay. You're very sick, and you might even get sicker."

Lane was not sure she had heard correctly. A fog began to infiltrate her head, and she had a hard time following the conversation. "What does that mean, exactly?"

Evelyn took her hand. "If you don't respond to treatment within the next forty-eight hours," she hesitated then continued, "you may not get better."

Lane didn't get any better, and eight days after entering the hospital she received a new heart. Now, more than a year later, all she had to show for her incredible ordeal was a scar and a bathroom cabinet full of immunosuppressant drugs.

Shaking off the melancholy that accompanied thoughts of her surgery, Lane brushed her hair, stepped into her shoes, and turned off the light in her bedroom. Walking into the kitchen, Lane exhaled deeply as she gathered her purse and searched for her keys. She hadn't been this nervous to be in the company of a woman in a long time. It had been years since she'd been out on a date, and she hoped she wouldn't make a fool out of herself because the rules had changed and no one had told her. What if Kyle wanted to sleep with her? Her doctor cleared her for sex months ago, but it was very different to have permission and to actually do it. She wasn't afraid of having a heart attack, but she hadn't told Kyle specifically about her surgery, and it wasn't as if she could hide her scar from a lover.

"Get a grip Lane. It's only dinner." Lane told her reflection in the mirror before she stepped into her garage.

❖

Kyle was sure she looked as ridiculous as she felt. Single women hanging out in the bar of a posh restaurant were typically looking for something other than their date to arrive. For at least the fifth time this evening, Kyle chastised herself for not having the guts to simply go to dinner with Lane like a grown up. She should have let Lane pick her up or at least volunteered to drive. It wasn't as if one meal together would signal a lifetime commitment, a white picket fence, and a minivan, for crying out loud. God forbid. She may have a child, but she'd rather walk than be seen in a *soccer-mom mobile*. A dinner was just that and nothing more. Normally, she fixed a light dinner and ate alone after Hollie had gone to bed. Why not enjoy a decent steak in conversation with a beautiful woman for a change?

Kyle frowned when she looked at her watch and saw that it was only four minutes since the last time the diamond encrusted dial winked back at her. Taking a deep breath, she glanced toward the front entrance and what she saw took her breath away.

Lane stood there in a dark green suit looking like she just stepped out of the latest issue of *Vogue*. Her hair was swept back off her face, earrings dangled from her ears, and her face was a mask of beauty. *My God, you're gorgeous, and I'm in big trouble here.* The thought had barely registered when Lane looked right at her and glided across the lobby to stop in front of her.

"Hi."

"Hi." Kyle was incapable of any coherent thought. Lane's eyes sparkled, but even in the dim lighting of the restaurant Kyle could see a wariness beneath the surface. She suspected Lane had picked up on her own trepidation of this evening and was being cautious. *Jesus, Kyle. The woman has been through hell and went out on a potentially embarrassing limb when she asked you out, and you treat her like a pending root canal. Your mother would be ashamed.*

Feeling like a real cad, as well as a fool, Kyle stepped away from the bar and said, "I've been looking forward to tonight."

She took in the skin exposed by Lane's open collar before lifting her eyes to Lane's face once more. The polite thing to do now was to pay a compliment, but Kyle didn't want to sound like she was saying what just anyone would say. She wanted Lane to know just how attractive she found her.

"You look beautiful," she said. "And not just because what you're wearing is stunning." Lane was totally unprepared for such a personal compliment, and she knew enough about women to know that it was not contrived flattery. Despite Lane's heels, Kyle was taller than her, and Lane had to look up to meet her gaze.

"Thank you," she said softly. "You clean up pretty well yourself."

Kyle was wearing charcoal trousers, a light gray silk shirt with a contrasting black jacket. Her dark hair was combed back from her face accentuating her green eyes which at that moment were focused totally on her. She looked polished, rugged and sophisticated all in one very attractive package. Anyone looking at her would assume she was a corporate executive and in Lane's mind she was every bit as successful.

"I hope you weren't waiting long."

"No, not at all," Kyle said. "I got here right before you did,"

Lane filed that polite lie away for future reference. She knew Kyle had been waiting longer than she implied because she'd sat in her car for at least fifteen minutes in plain view of the door as she racked her brain for an excuse to cancel the entire evening. If giving such short notice wasn't incredibly rude, she would have backed out. But taking a long look at the dashing detective standing tall in front of her made her glad she hadn't.

Their drinks had barely been served when the hostess arrived to show them to their table. After the waiter had taken their order, Lane twirled her wineglass in her fingers, suddenly nervous. "I guess this is the time when I'm supposed to ask you why you wanted to be a cop?"

"You could. But you could ask me something totally different too." Kyle sipped her drink. The bartender had made her a Grey Goose gimlet, and the two olives skewered on the toothpick was the crowning touch.

"All right, why did you accept my dinner invitation?"

"Jeez, and I thought I was a tough interrogator. You take no prisoners."

"I've come to realize that life's too short to pull any punches," Lane said matter-of-factly.

Kyle studied the woman seated across from her. The lighting in the dining room highlighted Lane's hair and softened her features. Her earrings danced when she spoke, and Kyle suddenly wanted to nibble on her perfectly shaped ears. "I will admit I was a bit surprised, but I guess I accepted because it sounded interesting. Why did you ask?"

"Ah, the leading question after the evasive answer." Lane laughed. "I guess I need to remember that you're a detective who spends every day getting people to confess."

Kyle enjoyed the tease. She had started to relax and simply enjoy her evening with Lane. She was surprised at how quickly her sense of humor surfaced, and she was not as tongue tied as she had been the last time they talked. She was beginning to feel like her old self again; the person she'd been before her life was upended by the death of her sister.

"I'm off duty, which means I left my rubber hose at home. Unless you want me to run back and get it." She set her drink down and started to rise from the chair as if she were going to do just that.

Oh this is going to be interesting. "Because I find you attractive and I'd like to get to know you a little better—without the clinking of orange juice glasses and the smell of coffee," Lane replied, alluding to the fact that the only times she and Kyle had ever talked were at The SandPiper.

The descriptor was no sooner out of Lane's mouth when Kyle made the connection and realized that was exactly the ambiance they were sharing now. Only this table was covered with a thick white cloth and Wedgwood china. Their glasses were filled with good wine, and coffee would be served in delicate cups, not the industrial coffee mugs at Lane's restaurant.

Lane melted into the laughing eyes across from her and pulled herself back. It wouldn't be smart to get too far involved until she had a better idea of where, if anywhere, they might go. "What if it were coffee at your breakfast table?" Kyle was not talking about one of the tables in The SandPiper, and from the candor in Lane's eyes, she knew it, too.

"Detective, I don't do the rubber hose on the first date."

The air around them filled with Kyle's laughter. "Well, I guess that takes all the awkwardness out of the good night kiss."

Their meals arrived, offering a temporary respite just as Kyle felt her pulse jumping erratically and her skin prickling with awareness. Dinner was delicious and included thick steaks, red wine, and lots of laughter. Kyle enjoyed the fact that Lane was a hearty eater, unlike many of the women she dated who were afraid to gain an ounce. She was also warm, witty, and intelligent. *And don't forget gorgeous.* She had a unique, almost reverent way of looking at life.

Part way through their meal, she asked Kyle, "What is the one thing that you are the most passionate about Kyle?"

Kyle's first instinct was to say that nothing mattered to her more than Hollie but she didn't. "Passionate? Hmm, let me think.

Other than my life and my family, which is a given, I'd say my job."

Lane looked at her as if to ask, "Really?"

"What, you don't believe me?"

"Why, do I have a reason not to?" Lane asked knowing she didn't but enjoyed teasing Kyle. She hadn't flirted with someone in a long time, and she had forgotten how fun it was.

Kyle put her hand over her heart in mock indignation. "I'm crushed. You think I'm full of bullshit."

"Trust me Detective, I do think you can be full of bullshit. That's how you're successful, bluffing some of the time. It's part of your job. Am I right?"

She was teasing but her voice held a distinct edge. Kyle didn't know the details about her breakup with her girlfriend, but it was obvious Lane had been deeply hurt. Wanting Lane to know she could trust her, she said, "Yes, bluffing is oftentimes part of the deal. But I'd never bullshit you. I'll lie about birthday presents and Christmas gifts, but I'll never lie *to* you."

Kyle's seriousness took Lane a little by surprise. Her eyes were grave, and an insistence in her tone gave the impression that she was trying to make a point. Lane wasn't sure how she could be so certain, but their conversation over dinner had cemented her belief that Kyle was an honest, decent woman.

After the waiter cleared their dishes, Lane thumbed through the dessert menu, trying to decide if she really wanted to eat more, or if she was simply making their evening last longer. Once she'd stopped feeling nervous, she'd enjoyed their time together even more than she'd expected.

Kyle sat back in her chair, her arms folded across her chest. "You can't actually have room for dessert?"

"My mom has a favorite saying that I learned at a very young age. 'There's always room for dessert.'" She closed the menu.

"I'll have the cheesecake." She flashed Kyle a look as if to say, "Want to make something of it?"

Kyle shook her head emphatically. "I wouldn't dream of standing between a gorgeous woman and her dessert."

"Why don't I believe you?"

"The part where I'll let you have your dessert, or the fact that I think you're a beautiful woman?" Lane blushed at her compliment which surprised Kyle. She thought Lane would have heard this all the time. "Don't you believe that you are?"

"Now how am I supposed to answer that?"

Kyle replied softly. "Just say thank you."

The candlelight flickered on Lane's face, softening the traces of sadness that Kyle's trained eye detected earlier. She wanted to make everything all right for Lane, and it frustrated her that she couldn't. What she could do, however, was make sure Lane knew just how attractive she thought she was. Her beauty was more than skin deep. She had a warmth about her Kyle had noticed the first day she met her. That friendliness spilled over into her work, and Kyle had often watched in fascination how Lane interacted with her customers. She seemed to truly care about them, especially the regulars. They were more than a check, they were people she was determined to please in her place of business.

"Thank you." Lane hesitated a few moments and then poked Kyle's hand with her fork. "But I'm still having the cheesecake."

Kyle laughed, releasing some of her tension as she motioned for the waitress and ordered for both of them. The restaurant's patrons had thinned leaving the women sitting almost alone.

"You know, most people aren't passionate about their life," Lane said after their desserts arrived. "It's a shame when they take so much for granted." She didn't want to be morose, but she couldn't help herself.

"That's a very insightful observation for someone who just ate her entire piece of cheesecake and half of mine as well."

They both laughed as the waitress refilled their coffee cups.

"I see death almost every day," Kyle said, sipping her coffee. "One minute you're eating popcorn in your living room and the next a bullet comes through your window and you're dead. Just like that." She snapped her fingers to make her point. "I always say 'I love you' to the people that matter to me. I think most cops do. You never know when you'll no longer have the chance."

Kyle's comment struck a chord with her. Her life had changed in an instant, and there was no going back. Her friends and family danced around the issue, but she faced it every time she took her clothes off. She experienced first hand how precious life was, and she cherished it every day. "So what is it about your job that drives you to do it every day?"

Kyle looked into her cup of coffee almost expecting the answer to be spelled out like the letters in alphabet soup. "It sounds kind of corny and trivial, but I think I make a difference." Lane seemed genuinely interested, so she continued, "The families of homicide victims need closure. They need to know that the guy that ripped their life apart will be held accountable. I try to provide that for them. Simple as that."

"I doubt if it's as 'simple as that,'" Lane said. She wasn't surprised by Kyle's understatement. The woman didn't seem the type to brag. "What you do is real, and serious. It's a big deal. I mean, you find people who kill other people, mothers and fathers and children. In my book, that's definitely a go-directly-to-heaven job."

Lane knew several cops, and she could not imagine what their lives must be like, seeing nothing but the sadness and the inhumane actions of people.

Kyle leaned back in her chair. "Cops are just people who

have a job just like everybody else. We get up every day, go to a job some of us are lucky enough to love, try to do the very best that we can and hopefully come home at the end of the day to start all over again the next morning." She realized that her tone was harsher than she had intended, yet she'd been trying to keep the conversation light.

"On the news the other day there was a lady who was arrested because she forgot her baby in the car and the kid died. How can they arrest her? Her child died, for God's sake. She has to go to jail too?"

Kyle's stomach jumped. She too had seen the news item and always hated stories like that. They made her job more difficult when she was coated with the broad brush stroke of simply being a cop. "She committed a crime."

Lane was flabbergasted. "What crime? Forgetfulness? Last time I checked I didn't think that was against the law."

Kyle told herself to stay calm. "Child endangerment."

"Oh for crying out loud. The stupid lady forgot her child was in the car. If anything, she should be charged for being stupid." Lane's voice softened. "She's suffered enough. She's going to have to live with her actions for the rest of her life."

This was one of the many things that frightened Kyle when Hollie first came home. She was not ready to be a mom, to be responsible for another human being. She was used to coming and going as she pleased, often times with little or no planning. She was terrified she would forget she was sleeping in the crib or in the back seat of her car.

"Yes, she will. People do stupid things all the time, and other people die because of it. They need to be held accountable." Kyle knew it wasn't as cut and dried as she made it sound.

"Accountable to whom? Society or God?"

"Yes."

The air was thick with tension. Lane was afraid that her stance on this issue was going to end their evening on a sour note. It might even end their seeing each other before it even began.

Kyle broke the silence. "How did we get on to something so serious?"

"It wasn't my doing, I just asked what made you tick."

"I guess it certainly isn't my biological clock." Kyle relaxed when Lane finally laughed.

Kyle stood and held Lane's chair. When she rose and moved ahead of Kyle, her perfume left a subtle trail that teased Kyle's senses. She liked the fragrance. *I love the way women smell.* She was so caught up in the pleasure of Lane's scent and the movement of her hips as she walked, that she almost ran into her when she stopped at her car.

"I had a wonderful time tonight, Kyle." Lane took control of their parting moment, leaning in to place a chaste kiss on Kyle's cheek. "I'd invite you over for a nightcap..."

"But you're not the rubber hose kind of girl," Kyle interrupted, relaxing a bit.

"No, I'm not. But with you, Detective, I could be," Lane said as she got into her car. "But I don't think you're ready for that. At least not yet." Lane drove away leaving Kyle rooted where she stood.

Kyle was still reeling from the unexpected kiss. It was the last thing she had expected, and it was over almost before she knew what was happening. Lane's lips were soft and warm and her breath on her cheek was feather-light the instant before she kissed her. For the second time in as many days she wasn't quite sure what just happened but she knew she wanted it to happen again.

CHAPTER FOUR

Sunday morning dawned bright and sunny, mirroring the disposition of the little girl with the warm brown eyes giggling in her mother's arms. On the weekends, when Kyle got Hollie out of her crib, she brought her back into bed with her for snuggles and giggles. Along with bedtime, it was the time of day she treasured the most. Right now, Hollie was tickling her and Kyle was doing a good job of exaggerating her laughter, much to the delight of her daughter.

Over a breakfast of Cheerios and bananas, Kyle kept up a stream of conversation with Hollie. They talked about their plans for the day which included a trip to the La Jolla petting zoo. Kyle couldn't remember how many times they had gone to the zoo, and she found joy and delight in the outing each and every time. *It's amazing what you see through the eyes of a child.*

Kyle's parents were waiting for them at the entrance to the zoo. Hollie wanted out of her stroller and in the arms of her grandmother the moment she saw her. Like most children her age, she adored her grandparents, and Michael and Constance Bain showed their love for her without reservation. Whether it was because she was their first grandchild, or because Hollie was their continued connection to Alison didn't matter. Watching them delight in the unconditional love and happiness of their granddaughter made Kyle smile, but she also felt a deep sadness.

Her parents had arrived at the hospital shortly after Hollie was born. Their faces had been pressed against the nursery window when Kyle walked up and stood beside them.

Her mother had chattered about their delayed flight and how the rental car place didn't have their reservation, and she thought they'd never get there. Rambling with excitement, she didn't seem to notice Kyle's subdued manner.

Kyle remembered exactly what she'd said as she tried to find the words to speak the unthinkable. "Allie was great and Hollie's perfect. She weighs five pounds and is eighteen inches long. She's passed all her newborn tests and other than being a little small, she's in perfect health." Her voice had cracked at the end of her statement.

That was when her mother finally fell silent. She looked frightened. "Kyle, what is it?"

Kyle froze, unable to find the words that she sometimes said every day. She had informed dozens of parents, children, and relatives of the death of a loved one, and she now knew exactly what they were going through. "It's Allie. She had complications after Hollie was born."

"What kind of complications?" Her father asked, drilling her with his eyes fighting the panic threatening to overwhelm him. He sensed there was something seriously wrong.

"She had a brain aneurysm probably brought on by the delivery," Kyle replied dully. "She hemorrhaged in her brain and they have her on life support. The doctors say she's probably brain dead."

After she'd broken the news, Kyle had comforted her parents as best she could. She'd only had a few hours to accept the news herself, and it felt as if her insides had been ripped out. Allie was her sister, her twin, and now half of everything she knew of herself was gone. She hovered on the edge of blackness, not wanting to turn around and not having enough guts to step forward.

❖

The Bain family strolled across the zoo grounds at a leisurely pace with Hollie perched on her grandfather's shoulders excitedly pointing at everything. Kyle and her mother drifted along behind them.

"Kyle, is everything all right? You seem a little distant this morning."

Her mother's question didn't surprise Kyle. Constance had a sixth sense when it came to her children, one that Kyle herself was developing with Hollie. The sun, and the fresh air, and the fact that she didn't have to watch Hollie like a hawk meant she could let her mind drift. When she let her mind wander, it usually filled back up with bits and pieces of cases she was working on, the empty refrigerator, or how many diapers were left in the box. But there was no room for mundane thoughts now; her head was spinning with visions of Lane. Lane walking through the door of the restaurant, Lane chatting with guests on the patio of her restaurant, Lane laughing, her hair shining in the moonlight, the look in her eyes just before she kissed her.

"Kyle?"

Answering her mother's question, she said, "Just thinking."

"Anything you want to share with your old mom?"

Kyle laughed and put her arm around her mother's shoulders. "You'll never be old, Mom, just wiser and more astute. You know when I was younger, I always hated that in you. Allie and I could never keep anything from you whether it was good or bad, and I hated it."

"And now?" her mother asked.

Kyle pulled her tighter. "I still hate it, but I appreciate your concern." She watched her father try to coax a duck to come closer to where he knelt with Hollie. "He's a great grandpa."

Kyle's mother smiled. "He always did have a way with the girls." She paused. "Speaking of girls, how's your love life?"

The change of subject made Kyle's head spin. Her mother seldom asked for details about her personal life. She produced a non-committal answer. "It's fine."

"Kyle, you're a single, attractive woman. It should be more than fine. It should be full and passionate."

"Mom!" Kyle gave her mother a startled sidelong glance. Constance was never so direct with her.

"Oh, please. Do you think I don't know about these kinds of things? I'm still madly in love with your father, and I don't see why those feelings would be any different between women. Alison's been gone for over a year now, Hollie is a wonderful, well adjusted child, Gretchen is a fabulous nanny and *you*," she emphasized with a well manicured finger poke in Kyle's chest, "need to get on with your life."

God I hope I'm as good a mother to Hollie as this woman is to me. Kyle often talked to her mother about the struggles she had juggling the priorities of her career and Hollie. She had yet to be convinced that Hollie would not grow up to be an ax-murderer if she occasionally went on a date.

"I did have dinner with someone last night," she said defensively.

Just thinking about her evening with Lane brought a smile to her face. Despite her misgivings, Kyle could not remember the last time she'd enjoyed herself so much. She'd thought about Hollie frequently at first, but when she finally relaxed about midway through the main course, Lane had held her undivided attention.

"And?"

"And it was okay." Kyle's answer was vague and knew it was not going to appease her mother. She was right.

"Kyle." Constance used the same tone she had when Kyle was a child.

"All right, all right, Mom, I had a good time. And you were right. Hollie didn't turn into an ogre because I spent a few hours with someone.

"So tell me about her."

Her mother's persistence surprised Kyle. She was a great mother and normally didn't pry into Kyle's life, but lately she had been dropping hints and asking not-so-subtle questions about her love life. And now, Kyle wanted to tell her. "Her name is Lane Connor and she owns The SandPiper down on Highway One. I've been going there for a few years, now. She used to be involved with someone and now she's not."

"I don't need to be a detective to be able to come to the conclusion that it was probably Lane who did the asking."

Kyle's silence prompted an "I'm your mother and know everything about you" look. "Where did you go?"

"The Stockyards. You know they recently re-modeled and it's great inside. Very beefy, yet cozy at the same time."

"What did she say when you told her about Hollie?" her mother asked, beaming in Hollie's direction. When Kyle didn't immediately reply, Constance rephrased her question. "You did tell her about Hollie, didn't you?"

Kyle quickly studied the map of the zoo pretending she hadn't heard.

"Kyle, it's a simple yes or no answer." Her mother sounded impatient.

"No, I didn't tell her, and it really isn't that simple."

"She's your daughter. I know I've been out of the dating scene for centuries, but don't people normally talk about their families when they get to know each other?"

"Yes mother, they do. But it just never came up. Lane didn't say anything about her family either." *Why am I being so evasive?*

"Why are you being so evasive Kyle?"

Jesus Christ, now she can read my mind! "It was just one meal. She didn't ask and I didn't volunteer."

Constance was frustrated. "Good God. 'Don't ask, don't tell' doesn't apply here." Her expression changed as an explanation dawned on her. "Are you afraid she won't be interested if she knows you have a child?"

"Of course not," Kyle replied quickly. "But if that is the case, then she wouldn't be the woman for me." She stopped talking when she realized that the comment made it seem like she was looking for a woman, which she was not. She took a deep breath to calm her nerves. "If and when I'm ready to begin seeing someone, Hollie and I are a package deal, no exceptions. I didn't tell her because it was just a dinner. No use spilling my life story if the woman turns out to be a dud."

"And did she?"

"Did she what?" Kyle was having a hard time following this simple conversation.

"Turn out to be dud? For heaven's sake Kyle, get your head in the game. If I didn't know any better I'd think you'd already fallen for this girl." Her mother lowered her sunglasses and peered at her. "Have you fallen for her?"

"Mom," Kyle dragged out. "I haven't fallen for her. For heaven's sake, we've only gone out to dinner. That's all. I've got nothing to hide." *Except my battle scars and fears.*

"Uh huh." Constance let the subject drop.

❖

The workweek began and when Kyle entered The SandPiper she literally ran into Lane just inside the front door. She reached out and grabbed her arms to keep her from toppling over. "Jesus, Lane, are you all right?"

Lane took a quick backward step. Kyle's hands felt like fire where they touched her skin. "I'm fine. I think you just surprised me more than anything."

"Are you sure you're okay?" Concern filled Kyle's eyes as they trailed down her body as if inspecting her condition.

Lane's breath caught in her throat before she could answer. "I'm fine."

She wasn't sure she would see Kyle again on a personal level, especially after their differences over whether or not the lady who left her child in the car should be prosecuted. It had been obvious that she wasn't comfortable with the change of direction in their relationship, but there were glimmers of contradiction in her demeanor. There were times when she was almost cold and impersonal and other times when the look of pure desire in her eyes shook Lane to the core. Lane suspected the detective was unaware that her eyes gave her away. Right now, they were dark and smoky with more than a hint of desire, and they prowled Lane's body with blatant sexual craving.

After that look, I'm really not fine, but I'm not going to tell you that. At least not yet. She took Kyle's hand. "Come on, let's get out of the entryway before someone else mows us down." She led Kyle to an empty table on the patio.

Kyle held the chair for her. "Thank you." Lane signaled Margo, the waitress, knowing that she would follow with coffee, but Kyle called Margo over instead.

"I'll have a raspberry-mocha frappuccino this morning." She glanced at Lane and was rewarded with a pleasantly shocked expression. Kyle knew she had pulled one over on her by asking for the same beverage Lane had made for her the other morning.

"I see you're expanding your beverage selection." Lane was thrilled Kyle remembered.

"It was time to step out on a limb and try something different." She was far too set in her ways. Kyle was talking about much more than changing her morning coffee.

"I had a wonderful time the other night."

"I did too. You're a charming dinner companion."

Margo set a colorful breakfast mug in front of Lane. Kyle immediately thought of the cups their coffee was served in after dinner. As she suspected, they were delicate china with handles so small she could barely get her fingers through. These she liked better.

"Charming? I don't think I've ever been called charming." Lane smiled, remembering that Kyle opened the door for her, and held her chair out for her. Kyle's actions were more than being polite. She was attentive and made her feel special.

Kyle chuckled. "Well, I suppose I could have said bright, intelligent, warm, and witty." Her eyes slowly scanned Lane's face. When she spoke again, her voice cracked a little. "And beautiful, don't forget beautiful. Would that have been more familiar?"

Kyle reached for her glass to regain her equilibrium. She'd made a split-second decision to come here in person. It would have been perfectly acceptable, and safer, to simply call Lane and thank her for dinner. Now that she was sitting across a table from Lane again, Kyle knew exactly why she had come. She wanted to see her again.

All coherent thought left Lane's brain when she met Kyle's eyes. Reflexively, she licked her lips and watched in fascination as Kyle's pupils darkened with barely restrained desire. An old familiar pulsing began in her crotch. A movement in the corner of her eye broke the spell, and she cleared her throat before answering, "I'm not used to being flattered, but thank you. I honestly didn't think I'd see you again."

It was Kyle's turn to be flabbergasted. "Why?"

"Because of my stupid comment about the lady and her baby. I thought I pissed you off."

Kyle smiled and relaxed. "No, you didn't piss me off, just a difference of opinion. Somebody once said you should never talk about religion, politics, or sex. There is no right or wrong position, and you will never convince someone to change theirs."

Lane started to giggle. "Speaking of sex and positions…" she hesitated enjoying the expression of fright on Kyle's face. "What are your thoughts on prostitution?"

Kyle was dumfounded at the change of subject. "As in have I ever paid for it? Or are you going to tell me you have?" Kyle was afraid to breathe.

"No silly. However, I do think it would be a lot simpler sometimes," Lane said, thinking out loud.

"How so?" Kyle was afraid of where this was leading but she couldn't help asking.

"It's kind of like shopping."

Kyle choked on her frappuccino.

"We buy everything else we want or need," Lane continued. "Why not sex?"

Was she always so practical? Kyle had often thought the same thing, especially when she was horny and no relief was in sight. But she was an officer of the law and it was her job to uphold it.

Uncomfortable, she replied, "I don't think I know how to answer that. Or what I should say, or shouldn't."

"Okay, I'll let you off the hook on this one."

"Are there going to be more?" Kyle asked tentatively.

Lane thoughtfully considered the question. "Probably."

Kyle wiped the spilled coffee from her chin. "Then could you possibly give me a little warning so I don't inhale my frappuccino again."

"Nah, I like to keep you hopping." Lanes eyes twinkled with mischief.

Kyle took several deep breaths to rein in her rapidly beating pulse. The ability for small talk deserted her. "I'd like to see you again." Her voice was husky.

"I'd like that too."

Once again, Kyle was drawn into Lane's bright blue eyes, losing herself in the depths of desire brewing in them. She had never been as attracted to a woman as she was to Lane, and certainly not this fast. *Was it only days ago that we saw each other again after so long?* The turn of events was thrilling and frightening at the same time.

"Do you dance?" Lane asked.

"Excuse me?" Kyle was not sure she heard her correctly.

"There's a dance at the Bay Club this weekend, and I'd like to go with you."

The Bay Club was a private club on the marina and admittance was by invitation only, the guest list a who's who of the lesbian community. The thought of being held in Kyle's arms on the dance floor turned the pulsing in Lane's crotch up several degrees. She was sure Kyle could sense her arousal.

Kyle was not certain her voice would work. The rapid beating of the vein in Lane's throat aroused her almost to the point of pain. *Jeez, this woman gets to me.* She dragged her eyes away as the waitress refilled Lane's coffee. Those few seconds enabled her to regain some sense of control, and she allowed herself to return Lane's candid stare. "Yes, I dance."

"Well?" Lane had to ask, unsure if Kyle had accepted her invitation or not.

"Sorry," Kyle replied embarrassed. "I'd love to go dancing with you."

Lane was intrigued as she watched Kyle struggle and then regain her balance. *This is an interesting woman.* A small smile formed on her lips. "The dance is Saturday. Are you free?"

"I am now." Kyle's mind shifted to babysitters. This was Gretchen's weekend off; she hoped her parents would be able to watch Hollie.

"Nine o'clock okay?"

"Would you like to grab some dinner before?" Kyle almost groaned aloud. *Before what? Before I take you in my arms and feel your body pressed against mine? Before I feel your arms around me and your breath in my ear? Before I watch your body move on the dance floor? Before I lose my mind?*

"That sounds great." Lane noticed Donna, her hostess, headed their way "I'm sorry Kyle, business calls. Would you excuse me?"

Kyle rose along with Lane and held her chair, as usual. "I've got to be going, too. How about I pick you up around seven? Chinese okay?"

Lane hated to leave so abruptly, but she knew that look in Donna's eyes and it meant trouble. "Perfect on both points. Here, let me write down my address." She pulled a business card and pen from her pocket. She looked up when Kyle chuckled. "What?"

"Well, I am a detective. I probably could have found out where you live."

"True, but this is much more personal, don't you think?" She held out the card with her address and phone number on the back.

"Yes, it is."

Their fingers touched as Kyle reached for the card. A bolt of pleasure traveled from her fingertips directly to her crotch.

Before she had a chance to think twice, Lane trapped her fingers between her own.

"Keep the streets safe, Detective."

With one last look, Lane walked away and Kyle was left at the table, alone and more aroused than she could remember being in years. The waves cresting on the beach below mimicked the pounding between her thighs, and watching Lane's ass as she retreated was blissful torment. She watched Lane lightly touch the shoulder of a customer Kyle knew was a regular. When she leaned down to talk to the man, her hair glinted in the morning sun. The thought of holding Lane in her arms was almost too much to bear. Kyle wondered how she was going to hold herself together until Saturday evening.

She started guiltily when her pager went off and reached for the phone on her belt. For a few seconds she forced herself to breathe slowly, then she dialed. She had no idea how she was going to carry on a normal conversation when all she wanted to do was make love to Lane.

CHAPTER FIVE

A woman named Gloria Faulkner was dead. After checking the detective's badge, the officer guarding the door of the apartment to which Kyle was summoned stepped aside to let her enter. Kyle was in full detective mode by the time she got to the rundown motel-turned-apartment. Far too many convictions were botched by inattentive investigators who were lazy or just didn't care. Kyle was not one of them. Her record as an investigator was spotless and her methods meticulous. Detective Bain was a prosecuting attorney's dream.

At first glance, Kyle wasn't sure if the condition of the apartment was the result of a struggle or simply that the tenant was a slob. Papers were strewn across every surface, and newspapers lay in piles around the room. Beer cans were everywhere, most crushed, lying on their sides, some in pools of their contents. Dirty dishes were piled in the sink, and take-out containers covered the rickety card table that occupied the center of the kitchen. Crime scene technicians were taking measurements and snapping pictures and barely glanced at her.

The smell was overwhelming as Kyle stepped further into the apartment. Death and decay accompanied by massive amounts of blood created a smell she would never forget for the rest of her life. Even though she knew the woman inside had probably been dead at least a week, Kyle kept her mind clear, not wanting to jump to any conclusions that might prejudice her judgment.

Swatting flies away, she stepped into the bedroom. The room was in shambles. The nightstand was on its side, a broken lamp on the floor, dresser drawers destroyed, their contents spilling out like a waterfall. Blood covered the bed. In some places it was minimal, in others a grotesque collage of shapes and thickness that had dripped on the floor at times masking entire areas of the thin, cheap carpet. But Gloria Faulkner, or what was left of her lying naked in the middle of the bed, was the reason she was here.

Out of the corner of her eye, Kyle saw Travis approach. When he'd called to give her the address of the homicide, Kyle had said that she would meet him there.

"Someday I'm gonna write a book where every baby born is given a 'be nice to people shot.'" Travis shook his head and sighed. "Sometimes this shit just gets to me."

Kyle nodded in silent agreement. Man's inhumanity to man was shocking, and just when she thought she had seen it all, another call came in. But no matter how disgusting and disheartening it could be, she wouldn't trade her job for anything. She loved what she did, and she loved using her brain to catch the bad guys. And she couldn't do it without the man standing next to her.

"If people were born nice we'd be out of a job," Kyle said. At this very minute, as she looked at Gloria Faulkner beaten to death, that concept didn't sound too bad, but she went on, teasing, "What would we do every day?"

"Play golf and watch *Judge Judy*."

"I don't play golf, and I think *Judge Judy* is ridiculous."

"Me too." Travis returned his attention to the deceased. "I guess we'd better get to work."

❖

It was late afternoon before Kyle had the opportunity to call her parents about watching Hollie on Saturday night. She left a message on their machine and promptly forgot about it as she investigated the death of Gloria Faulkner. So far, she and Travis had been able to piece together that Gloria was a twenty-four-year-old hooker with a nasty heroin addiction and that she worked the corner of Highland and Eighty-fifth Street, an area known for heavy prostitution activity. She had either opened her door to the wrong guy, or she knew her killer. Tomorrow they would get the medical examiner's report, which would pinpoint the time of death, and she and Travis would hit the streets again.

It was after seven before she felt comfortable enough with her progress on the Faulkner investigation to tidy her desk and go home. She called Gretchen before she left the station, asking her to keep Hollie up until she arrived.

Luck was with her and every stoplight was green, reducing her ride home to only fifteen minutes. She pulled into her garage and then hurried inside the house to see her little girl. Hollie's bedtime was seven-thirty, but Kyle wanted to spend just a few minutes with her daughter before she went to bed. When she was with Hollie, the ugliness of the world disappeared in those big brown eyes and butterfly kisses. Three yawns later Hollie was sleeping soundly in her arms. She gently laid the child in her crib, turned on the baby monitor and left the Winnie the Pooh room.

Kyle was staring at her dinner as it bubbled in the microwave when her phone rang.

"Hi, Mom." Kyle answered eagerly when the caller ID displayed the familiar number.

"Hi, sweetie. We got your message and thought we'd wait till you got Hollie down for the night." Kyle's parents knew how little time she had to spend with her daughter and hesitated to intrude on their precious time.

"She just went down. I had Gretchen keep her up a little late so I could see her."

"Bad day?"

That was her mother's way of asking if there was yet another murder for her daughter to investigate. "Yeah." That's all Kyle ever said. Her home was her sanctuary from the ugliness of the world she saw every day, and she refused to bring it inside. "Can you watch Hollie Saturday night?"

Kyle held her breath, anticipating the third degree she would receive from her mother since their mother-daughter chat at the zoo. She was relieved when it didn't transpire.

"Oh that's perfect, honey. We're hosting the bridge club this week, and I was just saying to your father that we need to show off our little girl to our friends. What time do you want to bring her by?"

"Is six too early?" It only took ten minutes to get to her parents house, but it would take another twenty to get to Lane's.

"Do you want to join us for dinner?" Constance asked.

Kyle smiled at the familiar request. No matter how old she was, her mother thought the only good meal Kyle ever ate was one served by her mother, preferably in Constance's kitchen.

"Sorry, Mom. I'd love to, but I have dinner plans." Kyle hoped she wouldn't need to reveal too much more to her perceptive mother.

"Anyone special?" Constance asked with not a shred of subtlety.

Kyle laughed. She knew she wouldn't get off the hook without a question or two. "Mom, you really should work on your interrogation techniques. You reveal yourself far too easily."

"That's your job dear. Mine is being a mother and I can ask whatever I want. So are you going to answer my question?"

Kyle shook her head as she poked her fork into the hot

lasagna, releasing a funnel of steam from the soft pasta. "Yes, Mom, I'm going to dinner with Lane."

"That's wonderful Kyle. You need to get out more."

Kyle didn't argue on this point. "You're right."

"Why don't we keep Hollie for the night," her mother suggested happily. "That way you won't have to disturb her to take her home."

"You sure you don't mind?" Kyle wondered why she even asked that question. Her parents jumped at every opportunity to spend time with their grandchild.

"You should know better than that. We love spending time with Hollie. Why do you think we didn't move to Florida when we retired?"

Moving to Florida was a running joke in their family even though Kyle knew her parents were not the type to sit around and play canasta and bingo three times a week. "Thanks Mom. Hollie loves being with you and Dad, too." They chatted for a few more minutes and by the time her mother hung up, Kyle's dinner was cool enough to eat.

❖

The week dragged like molasses in winter for Lane. Her thoughts kept drifting to Kyle and their date on Saturday. She expected the dance would be as enjoyable as their dinner together, but she was nervous about what would come after. She had no idea why she'd asked Kyle to go dancing. She hadn't danced in years. Her ex, Maria had been self conscious about her dancing ability and would not set foot on the dance floor until she'd had at least four cocktails. Maria's coordination then disappeared along with her inhibitions, making the entire effort pointless.

Every morning that week Lane waited expectantly for Kyle

to make her usual appearance on the patio of the The SandPiper. By Friday she was on pins and needles, afraid that Kyle was going to cancel their date, and when she called to confirm later in the day, Lane finally relaxed. She was thrilled at the excitement in Kyle's voice and the long awaited knock on her front door could not come soon enough.

This evening Kyle was wearing impeccably cut tan trousers, a tan print silk shirt, and a dark brown double breasted blazer. "Stunning" was the only word that came to Lane's mind. There was an equally descriptive word that came to mind when she felt the rhythm of her blood pound between her legs and that word was "lust." Lane realized that she was staring, and Kyle was still standing on her porch.

"I'm sorry, come in," she stammered, embarrassed by her reaction and lack of manners.

"Thanks. These are for you." *No shit, Sherlock.*

"They're lovely." Lane accepted the bouquet of daisies and stepped away from the door as Kyle crossed the threshold. "I can't remember the last time a woman brought me flowers." *Other than on my death bed. And then she left. Thanks, Maria. Very classy.*

"That's a shame. A beautiful woman should always receive flowers."

"Thanks." Lane knew she was blushing slightly and turned away to conceal the fact. "Come in the kitchen while I put these in some water."

Lane's reaction to the flowers washed away the uncertainty Kyle had experienced standing in the flower shop on her way over. She must have been there fifteen minutes trying to decide if she should even bring flowers. In her mind bringing flowers to a woman you were dating was expected. What troubled her was whether she was ready to cross that line from dinner to dating.

The line was more like the Grand Canyon as far as Kyle was concerned, and she could only imagine what it would feel like if she made it to the other side.

"Wow." Kyle made a slow circle impressed by the kitchen that was almost as large as her living room. "I don't know why I'm surprised, you do own a restaurant so it's probably safe to assume that you're a pretty good cook."

Lane laughed as she took the flowers out of the paper and laid them on the counter. "I can see now why you're a detective."

Kyle smiled. "Touché." Kyle liked Lane's sense of humor.

"Do you bring flowers to all your dates?" Lane froze not believing what she just asked.

"Not recently." Kyle answered tentatively. This certainly was not a question she expected.

To Lane there was no turning back so she jumped in with both feet. "And why is that?"

Kyle wondered where this conversation was heading. "I haven't gone out much."

Lane was surprised at the admission. Kyle was very attractive and almost certainly had women falling all over her. "I can't imagine you spending many evenings alone." Kyle's eyebrows raised in tandem. "I mean, look at you. You're, you're…" Lane gestured with her hands palms up struggling with the right phrase. "Hot," she finally blurted out. It was the only word that adequately described Kyle.

Lane's description of her was more appropriate to the way she was feeling than the way she thought she looked. She was glad that Lane found her attractive, but if she didn't stop looking at her like she was right now, Kyle was afraid she would spontaneously combust.

"Let's just say I've had other priorities occupying my time." Kyle glanced at the clock on the wall confident the priority she referred to was fast asleep in her parent's house.

Kyle wasn't quite ready to answer personal questions but knew she would have to sooner or later if she continued to see Lane. Lane reached to pull a vase down from above the stove, and Kyle caught a glimpse of bare thigh, her mouth suddenly very dry. She tilted her head just a bit to get a better view and it was at that moment, Lane turned around and caught her looking.

"You're busted, Detective." Lane teased.

Kyle laughed, her gaze returning to the slit in the soft skirt Lane was wearing. "Guilty as charged ma'am. However I have the right to remain silent because anything I say you might hold against me. And let me tell you, the way you look tonight you can hold any part of you, I, uh, mean anything against me you'd like."

Kyle's slip of the tongue was intentional. She was not usually this bold in conveying her appraisal of women, but she had never seen a woman as striking as Lane was tonight.

The look in Kyle's eyes could not be mistaken for anything other than passion, and it took Lane's breath away. She was simultaneously thrilled and frightened and didn't know which one to follow. She took the safe way and chose both.

"I'll remember that." She winked at Kyle and touched her arm as she walked to the chair that held her jacket. "Ready?"

Several different scenarios flashed through Kyle's mind as she helped Lane with her jacket. She let her hands linger on her shoulders after the garment was in place. She leaned in close to her ear. "Whenever you are."

❖

Dinner was at a new Chinese restaurant that Lane recommended. As they sipped their tea, Kyle could not keep her eyes off Lane sitting across the table. She was ravishingly beautiful, and if she wasn't careful, that might be how the evening would end, with Kyle ravishing her. *If I make it that long.* The candle light flickered on Lane's face, revealing only a hint of makeup. She had pulled her hair back into a French knot accentuating her long throat. Kyle almost choked when she saw Lane swallow.

"Kyle?"

"Yes."

"Your dinner's here." Lane was amused that her date didn't appear to have noticed the waiter hovering by her right arm delicately balancing the numerous plates and bowls.

Kyle jerked as Lane's words permeated her head that was thick with desire. "Sorry," she apologized to the waiter. She gathered herself as he arranged the plates and handed her chopsticks. "Thank you."

After a few moments Kyle realized that Lane was frowning and not eating. "Is there something wrong with dinner?"

"No, I'm sure it's very good." Lane felt foolish. "I never mastered the use of chopsticks." She looked around the table for any sign of a fork.

Kyle laughed. "You own a restaurant and you don't know how to use chopsticks? Isn't that kind of like not knowing how to boil water?" She knew Lane would not be offended by her teasing.

"You're not as good of a detective as I thought. I don't own a Chinese restaurant. The closest thing I have to Chinese food is hot tea." Lane tried her best to keep from smiling but failed miserably.

"Here, let me show you." Kyle spent the next few minutes showing Lane how to maneuver the ancient eating utensils, all to no avail. Lane had more food fall back in her plate than in her mouth.

Frustrated at her inability to use the utensils, Lane muttered,

"I'm going to starve to death."

"Here." Kyle reached over the small table with a juicy piece of chicken clasped tightly in her chopsticks. "Open."

Lane complied and Kyle unerringly placed the meat in her mouth.

"Mmm, either that's delicious or I'm so hungry from the effort to try to eat anything is good." Lane mimicked Kyle's fingers working the chopsticks once again and failed.

"I admire your persistence. Open." This time there was a mixture of rice and vegetables with the meat. "You'll get the hang of it. It took me weeks to figure it out."

"That's comforting," Lane replied with her mouth full of food. "I'd rather have a fork."

Kyle laughed as she took a bite for herself. She gathered up more food. "But this is much more fun, don't you think?"

Mischief danced in her eyes, and Lane decided to play along in a slightly different way. She slowly opened her mouth and sensuously extended her tongue to lightly sample the flavor of the chicken dumpling Kyle offered her. Her stomach flipped when Kyle's eyes darkened and slightly glazed over. *Bingo!* When Kyle offered another piece, Lane seductively took the dripping meat from the chopsticks.

Holy Christ! Kyle stopped breathing when Lane's tongue peeked out and slowly licked the remaining juice off her lips. Her blood roared in her ears and her crotch throbbed as she imagined that tongue in a much different place. Her body flushed with desire.

"Kyle? Are you all right?"

Are you kidding? Fuck no! Kyle blinked several times to clear the erotic vision. "Yes, I'm fine."

Liar. Lane waited expectantly for another bite and this time noticed a slight trembling of Kyle's outstretched hand. Lane locked eyes with the detective who was valiantly attempting to disguise her arousal. *The eyes. Your eyes give you away.* She didn't break contact until she had swallowed the entire delicious morsel.

"You're right, this is much more fun than a boring fork."

A small twitch registered under Kyle's right eye, the only physical indication that she'd heard her sultry response. Lane didn't pick her chopsticks up again for the remainder of the meal. If Kyle's response to her teasing was any indication of what was to come, Lane couldn't wait to get her on the dance floor.

CHAPTER SIX

Kyle felt the pulse of the music before she opened the door to the exclusive Bay Club. Her trained eye detected several professional security guards discretely stationed around the parking lot, and she relaxed a little. She reached for her wallet to pay the cover charge.

Lane placed her hand over Kyle's. "No, it was my invitation, I'll pay." The expression on her face clearly said that there would be no further discussion.

They stepped inside and Kyle felt all eyes turn their way. The familiar feeling of being on display when she entered a bar, any bar, returned. The Bay Club was no exception. Lane must have felt the overt scrutiny too because she stepped closer and slipped her hand into Kyle's.

"Something to drink?" Kyle asked, leading them toward one of many bars strategically placed around the large room.

Lane noticed more than a few women casually watching her date cross the crowded room. Kyle appeared to be oblivious of the appreciative stares, but Kyle's fingers clasped her hand tighter. She didn't know if Kyle intended to signal to the women in the room that she was with Lane, but her possessive body language just felt right. When Kyle released her hand to pay for their drinks, Lane felt like she had lost her lifeline.

Kyle handed Lane her beer and spotted an empty table far

from the stage where the speakers towered over the dancers. She reclaimed Lane's hand and confidently headed to the table. Kyle moved the only stool so it faced the dance floor and indicated for Lane to sit. She stepped beside her so that she too could see the door. She scanned the room and took note of several prominent women from the area. The dance floor filled up as the band played a variety of music.

"See anything interesting?" Lane asked.

Kyle's eyes never stopped moving as she continually surveyed her surroundings and for some reason, her vigilance made Lane feel safe. The only exception was when Kyle dropped her gaze to meet Lane's. Those long, hot stares made Lane feel like she was the only woman in the room, and the one Kyle desired.

"I see a spot on the dance floor that has our name on it." Kyle put her beer on the table and held out her hand. "Shall we?"

Lane's pulse jumped to a rapid tempo, and her mouth was suddenly dry with anticipation. Her hand trembled slightly as she placed it in Kyle's. "Yes, definitely."

Kyle was a fabulous dancer, a few inches taller than Lane, and their bodies fit together perfectly. The band switched to a country song and they straddled each other's legs allowing them to glide. Lane's eyes were in direct line with Kyle's mouth. *Trouble,* she thought as Kyle's arm tightened around her and they moved effortlessly across the dance floor. Kyle's steps were so sure that Lane didn't have to concentrate on her own. Losing herself in the music and the warm strength of Kyle's body, she allowed her mind to drift.

She hadn't realized how much she missed human contact, intimate human contact until Kyle held her in her arms. Her friends and family hugged her when they got together, but those were perfunctory, simple, platonic hugs. She thought hard to remember the last time Maria held her tenderly. It had to have been months before she became ill, and a fleeting moment of emptiness washed over her because at the time Lane hadn't even realized it was happening.

Lane focused on Kyle and how sexy she felt in her arms. Could it have only been a little more than a week since Kyle came back into her life? It seemed like much longer, like she had always been part of her life. Lane often thought she actually had two lives. Her first life was before she fell ill, in which she took everything for granted and in which she and Maria would grow old together. Her second life began the day she woke up after her transplant. She realized that she had been given a second chance and had vowed to embrace every day.

Lane remembered that she always hated those first few dates with someone new. The small talk and getting to know each other, each woman on her best behavior. It was always such an effort, and most of the time she remembered it was a waste of time. But she didn't feel that way about Kyle. It was as if they had done all of that and knew enough about each other to simply just be comfortable with each other. Lane knew that wasn't true, she hardly knew anything about Kyle, but it felt as if she did. There was a connection that had sprung to the surface in her new life, and being with Kyle just felt right. And being in her arms was more than just right. It was perfect.

"You're an excellent dancer."

"Thank you, I'll pass the compliment on to my mother. She insisted that I take lessons when I was in the seventh grade. It was *the* most humiliating time in my life." Kyle smiled at the memory of her awkward adolescence. Her attraction to girls was still a mass of confusion, and all she could do during dance lessons was fight the boys who partnered her for the lead and step on their toes.

"I never would have imagined anything humiliating

happening to you. You're always so calm and self assured."

Kyle laughed. When it came to Lane she was anything but. "I was thirteen years old, taller than everyone in the school and had stringy hair and big feet. And I had just discovered I liked girls and not boys. Needless to say it was a time in my life that I am very glad is over."

Lane put some distance between them running her eyes over her dance partner, liking what she saw. "Well, I must say you certainly outgrew all of that."

Kyle laughed, slightly uncomfortable at the compliment. Missing the feeling of Lane's body against hers, Kyle pulled her back into her embrace.

Four songs later, Kyle led Lane back to the table. Lane settled on the stool and crossed her legs affording Kyle a view of a dozen inches of tanned skin. Kyle almost reached out to touch the tantalizing expanse but stopped herself and instead signaled the waitress for another round of drinks.

They danced together throughout the evening. Holding Lane in her arms was both a tortuous experience and the most exhilarating Kyle had experienced in a long time. Her pulse beat in direct contrast to the speed of the songs they danced to. The slower the song, the faster her blood raced through her veins, fanning the flame smoldering inside her. She was a master at controlling her outward emotions, but the desire raging inside was another matter altogether. She was acutely aware of the smell of Lane's shampoo and the way their bodies fit as if they were made for each other. During one particular ballad, Kyle caught their reflection in the mirrors that adorned the south wall and missed a step. They both stumbled, and she pulled Lane closer to keep her from falling. "Sorry."

Lane didn't reply. The breath was sucked out of her lungs by a jolt of desire that exploded in her groin. Her legs trembled and she could feel her panties soaking. Acutely aware of Kyle's body against hers, she tried to use the dance steps to disguise her physical reactions. She thought about making some excuse and going back to their table, but her mouth refused to form the words. She was in no position to fight the nearness even if she wanted to.

A little after midnight, Lane was light-headed but didn't know if it was from the physical exertion of dancing or simply from being held in Kyle's arms. They stepped back from one another in a break between songs. Lane's chest rose and fell with each ragged breath. "One final dance?" Kyle's green eyes bored into her own all the way to her soul.

Lane stepped into the waiting arms. "Only if you promise it's the last dance for tonight, and we'll come back again."

"I think I can honor that."

Their bodies moved in rhythm. Lane felt warm breath caress her ear and tickle her neck. She molded her body into Kyle's and was rewarded with a low moan of desire. Kyle's thigh was pressed tightly between her legs as their hips worked sensuously, one against the other. Lane's already hard nipples became almost painful as they brushed against the hard chest in front of her.

Kyle felt Lane's body react and gently cupped her face. She caressed Lane's cheek with the back of her hand as the tempo of the music slowed. Her thumb quivered across Lane's lips. "You're very beautiful."

Lane could only watch Kyle's lips, and they drew nearer. "I bet you say that to all the girls."

"Only to those I'm about to kiss." An instant later she lowered her mouth to the lips that had tormented her all evening. Lane's kiss was softer than she could ever have imagined and so responsive Kyle tentatively deepened their kiss until she knew she needed to stop or take their encounter elsewhere.

Rockets exploded behind Lane's eyes. She had never experienced this reaction when kissing someone and was almost overcome with the sensation. Kyle was an excellent, considerate kisser and did not try to overpower her with lips and tongue. Lane relaxed into the embrace and hoped it would go on forever, but Kyle pulled away much too soon.

"The song is over." Her voice was husky and unsteady.

The statement took a moment to penetrate her passion-clouded mind, and Lane slowly opened her eyes. Looking around, she was embarrassed to see that they were the only couple left on the dance floor. Her gaze returned to Kyle, meeting brightly burning eyes that contained a hint of sparkle. The kiss had left her so breathless she had a hard time responding to Kyle's comment.

"Maybe there'll be an encore."

Kyle's eyebrow quirked upward at the dual meaning conveyed by both her words and her tone. "I think there's more where that came from." She took Lane's hand and led them back to their table, thankful that her outward poise concealed the fact that she could barely put one foot in front of the other.

Kyle didn't sit but stood behind her as Lane sank down gratefully on the stool. Her warm breath caressed Lane's ear. "You're a wonderful kisser," she said softly. *That's an understatement.* Kyle could have died right there and been happy.

Lane chuckled and tilted her head so Kyle had better access to her sensitive neck. "I could be witty and say that my mother insisted I take kissing lessons when I was in the seventh grade."

"Would that be the truth?" Kyle started to nibble on the smooth neck under her ear.

At the first brush of her lips, Lane drew a quick breath. "No."

"Don't lie to me. I have ways of making you talk, you know."

Kyle paid particular attention to a very sensitive spot just under Lane's left ear.

Lane leaned into the hard chest against her back. "If you keep doing that I'll tell you the name of my pet goldfish I had when I was eight."

"Maybe I should use this technique on everyone I have to interrogate. It appears to be quite effective."

"You want the truth?" Lane turned a little to look up at the woman making her shiver. "The truth is that I want you to kiss me again." She wrapped her arms around Kyle's neck and buried her hands in her hair. A moan came from Kyle when she opened her lips. The sensation of Kyle's tongue entering her mouth for the first time was almost enough to send her over the edge. *From just a kiss?* She swayed into the strong arms that supported her, closing the gap between them even more.

Kyle fought for control as Lane responded to her kisses. Her hands moved slowly over Lane's back in soft caresses and eventually settled on her butt.

"Ladies?"

Kyle recovered first and broke away. Breathing heavily, she glared at one of the bartenders.

"Sorry to interrupt, but it's closing time."

Lane eased her arms from around Kyle's neck and slowly let her hands run down the front of her shirt to come to rest on her thighs. "Guess we'd better go before they call the cops."

Kyle laughed. "No, we don't want a cop around to spoil the fun."

Lane looked her straight in the eyes. "Actually, I'm having a lot of fun with a cop."

"Then let's go have some more fun." Kyle placed a chaste kiss on Lane's lips and helped her to her feet.

Lane followed her wordlessly out the door and through the

parking lot to Kyle's Saab, one of the few remaining vehicles in the lot. She made sure her body brushed Kyle's as she slid into the passenger seat.

Kyle's body immediately went into overdrive and she moaned. "You don't play fair."

"I don't have to. I'm playing with a cop."

Kyle moaned again in mock frustration and put the top down on the powerful car. She had left Hollie's car seat with her parents just in case they wanted to take her out for ice cream. The cool breeze caressed her heated skin but did nothing for the searing heat between her legs. She held Lane's hand as they drove slowly through the summer night. Out of the corner of her eye she could see Lane's head tipped back against the headrest, her eyes scanning the cloudless sky. There was a full moon, and the reflection of the city lights cast a soft glow on the smoothness of her throat. Kyle's stomach churned and her fingers twitched at the thought of caressing that vulnerable flesh.

Lane broke the silence. "I can't remember the last time I closed a bar."

"I can't remember the last time I made out in a bar." Not that she was a reluctant partner in the debauchery.

Lane slowly turned her head, teasing, "Am I a bad influence on you detective?"

"No." Kyle forced her eyes to stay on the congested road. Lane rubbed her thumb seductively on the top of Kyle's hand in a manner that drove her to distraction.

"Am I leading you astray?" Lane offered an innocent smile.

"You may lead me many places Ms. Connor, but astray is not one of them."

"Is that a proposition? Because if it is I may have to call the police."

"Professionally speaking, I prefer to call it a proposal—

proposition sounds so illegal. And even though I like girls, spending the night in a jail cell full of them is not exactly what I had in mind."

Lane shifted in her seat so that she was regarding her date directly. "And just what *exactly* did you have in mind?"

"I'll never tell. I'm a trained investigator. I know all the tricks to make people talk, but my lips are sealed." It had been ages since Kyle blatantly flirted with a woman like this. She'd forgotten how exciting it was, and how arousing. *Like I need any help with that.*

"What if I promise to use *my* rubber hose?"

Kyle laughed as she remembered that was her line the first time they had gone out to dinner. "Why am I not surprised? I already know you don't fight fair. But I bet mine is bigger than yours."

Lane cursed the fact that she was wearing a longer skirt and not a mini that was back in style. She moved Kyle's hand closer to the vee between her legs that was clamoring for attention. "You disappoint me, Detective. As worldly and sophisticated as you are, I would have thought you believe size doesn't matter."

"The only people who say that don't have a big one." Kyle coasted the car to a stop at an intersection. When she moved her hand, she watched the expression on Lane's face change. The light teasing was quickly replaced with raw hunger. She leaned in fully intending to kiss Lane and was thrilled when Lane met her more than halfway. The kiss started tentatively and when Lane increased the intensity, Kyle pressed her hand into her crotch. Lane gasped, and at the same time, a horn sounded from the car behind them. The light was green.

"That's twice tonight you've been caught." When Kyle pulled away from their kiss she did not pull her hand away from its present position between Lane's legs.

Kyle smiled thoughtfully. "Hmm, I seem to be running as fast as you can catch me. I wonder what that means?"

"That means you'd better drive faster."

Kyle did.

❖

Kyle smoothly pulled the car into Lane's driveway. She turned off the engine but did not put the top up on the convertible.

"Aren't you coming in?" Lane was confused. The activities of the past few hours clearly indicated they would spend the night together, at least it did to Lane. Apparently she was wrong.

Kyle didn't know what to say. She wanted to make love with Lane, but she suddenly realized she couldn't. Not tonight, anyway, and not until she told her about Hollie. It wouldn't be right to lead her somewhere when she had no idea there was something waiting for her at the other end. And Kyle wasn't quite ready to show her the map. She cursed herself for letting things get this far, but she'd been unable to stop herself the instant Lane stepped into her arms.

"Kyle?" Lane's heart dropped as her desire was quickly replaced with confusion and what could be described as pain. She didn't understand the quick change of events. She felt sure it wasn't anything she did, but she had no idea what had caused it.

Kyle ran her hand over her eyes which were suddenly very tired. "Lane, I'd be lying if I said I didn't want to, because God knows I do. But…"

"But what?"

Kyle struggled to find the right words. "I can't, not tonight. I'm sorry if I led you to believe otherwise." *What a jerk, Bain.*

Lane took a deep breath to calm the anger that was rising in her. "It's all right. I think we'd both better slow down a bit."

Wanting to hide her hurt, she reached for the door handle.

Kyle's heart dropped, and she was in a near panic fearing that she had blown it with this wonderful woman. "Lane," she begged softly and lightly put her hand on Lane's thigh, "Please, I'll get the door."

Lane didn't know what she'd expected Kyle to say but it certainly wasn't that. She had crashed from overwhelming joy to an emptiness she didn't want to think about. She dropped her hand and sat back against the seat.

Kyle hesitated a moment, caught between wanting to take this wonderful woman into her arms and wanting to tell her about Hollie, both of which she knew she shouldn't do. So she did the only thing she could, she got out of the car, opened Lane's door and held out her hand.

Lane looked at the hand offered and then into the eyes of the woman extending it. She knew it was more than a polite gesture. Somehow she knew that it was a peace offering of sorts. An offering to bridge the gap that had suddenly sprung up between them. Lane read the hope and fear as it crossed Kyle's face. Making a decision she knew she wouldn't regret, she smiled, took the hand and unexpectedly stepped into Kyle's arms and kissed her.

Their lips joined with the same intensity and passion as they experienced earlier in the evening, and when Lane broke away they were both breathing hard. "If tonight was any type of a preview of what's to come, you definitely will be worth the wait Detective. But let me tell you right now, I'm not known for my patience. Now walk me to the door."

Kyle was stunned at the quick turn of events but knew a command when she heard one. "Yes ma'am."

CHAPTER SEVEN

It was raining heavily and Kyle was running late. She was usually at her desk by eight, but this morning Hollie decided to take her first steps, and she was not going to miss the milestone simply to get to work. Travis usually didn't come in until after nine, and none of the other detectives had arrived, so Kyle had some privacy in the squad room when she sat down. She picked up the phone and dialed the number printed on the card in her hand. After several rings it was answered by the one voice she wanted to hear.

"Good morning," she replied quickly. "It's Kyle."

Lane's blood immediately heated and raced through her body. "Good morning." Her voice equaled the warmth pulsing through her veins.

"How are you this morning?"

"Tired. How are you?" Lane had been unable to sleep after their evening together, and the few hours she did sleep last night certainly didn't make up for it.

"Tired? Why are you tired? Have a busy weekend?" Kyle smiled as she leaned back in her chair and put her feet on her desk.

Lane was standing at the hostess stand, and it didn't afford her any level of privacy. Asking Kyle to hang on, she quickly crossed the twenty feet to her office and closed the door behind her. She picked up the receiver, cleared her throat, and released the hold button. "Yes, tired, and yes I did have a busy weekend. I seem to have stayed out quite late, or was it quite early, with a woman who literally swept me off my feet."

Kyle laughed remembering the feel of Lane in her arms and just how light on her feet she actually was. "Really? Swept you off your feet, huh?"

"Yep. She was a marvelous dancer. She was a strong lead, could dance to just about anything and was devilishly attractive. I practically had to fight the girls off with a stick." Lane had been approached in the ladies room by a woman who wanted to ask Kyle to dance, but she was smart enough to ask Lane if she and Kyle were *together*. The woman went away disappointed.

Laughter filled the earpiece. "A big stick?"

"Very. She could have had any woman in the joint." Kyle may have been aware of her magnetism, but she never gave any indication she noticed any of the sultry looks directed her way.

"Aren't you exaggerating a little bit? *Any* woman in the room?"

"Yep, even the straight ones. They couldn't take their eyes off her, either." This was also one hundred percent true. Kyle radiated power and sensuality and carried herself with confidence. Between these attractive characteristics and a drop-dead gorgeous body, she was definitely the hottest woman at the dance.

"Okay, now I know you're pulling my leg." Kyle was beginning to feel uncomfortable, and she took a more serious tone.

"Kyle, do you have any idea what you do to women?" *God, how could she not know?*

"There's only one woman I'm interested in doing something to." Even though she was still alone in the office, Kyle dropped her voice.

An immediate gush soaked Lane's panties from Kyle's comment. Her hands started to shake and her breathing became shallow. She sat up straighter in her chair in a failed attempt to regain control over her body, but all she succeeded in doing was pressing her throbbing crotch tighter against her panties.

"Oh man." Lane wasn't aware she spoke the words until Kyle responded.

"No…oh, woman." Kyle felt the sexual tension through the phone lines. The events of Saturday night had haunted her all day Sunday. Physically, she'd kept busy, but with the exception of playing with Hollie, the day was mostly spent in generally mindless activity. Kyle was not able to pinpoint when she'd crossed the line from simply being interested in Lane to wanting her. She wrapped her hand around the receiver, and her fingers tingled with the memory of the feel of Lane's skin. She could no longer maintain her casual, relaxed position, and her feet hit the floor with a thud.

"Kyle…I…" Lane knew what she wanted to say but wasn't able to form the words. She wanted Kyle, there was no doubt about it, and it was apparent by Kyle's reactions Saturday night that she wanted her just as much.

Kyle was distracted when the precinct captain entered the room and motioned her to his office. *Shit.* "Lane?"

"I want to see you again."

"I want to see you again too." The captain could wait. That thought was very unlike her.

"What are you doing tomorrow night?"

"I've got the duty, but other than that I'm free."

Lane looked puzzled. "The duty?"

"It's kind of like being on call. If there's a homicide or a suspected homicide I'm called. We rotate the duty during the week so one of us doesn't get stuck getting up in the middle of the night all the time."

Kyle's description was confusing. "How do you have a suspected homicide? Aren't they either dead or not dead?"

Kyle laughed at the innocence of the question. "I've never had anyone ask that question, but it's a good one. A suspected homicide is one where there's a doubt whether or not there was any foul play in the death. Like a homicide that is staged to look like a suicide."

Lane nodded her understanding. "So when you have the duty, what exactly does that mean?"

"It just means that if I'm called I have to go. We may have to end the evening early, and I'd have to take you home. Then again, my pager may not go off at all."

Lane thought about that for a moment. "Let's live life on the edge. Let's go out."

"I knew there was a reason I liked you. What would you like to do?"

"You're gonna think it's corny."

"And why would I think that? Is it?" Kyle's curiosity was always in high gear and went into overdrive when it came to this woman.

"Not to me."

"Then not to me either."

"I'd like to go to the boat show," Lane said. "And tomorrow is the last night."

Kyle laughed. "Jeez for a minute there I thought you were going to ask if we could do something corny like hold hands and walk on the boardwalk." There was nothing she'd like better than to hold hands and walk with this woman.

Lane was relieved. "We can save that for another time. I really want to see the boats."

"All right, how about I pick you up at six? We can grab a bite somewhere or eat overpriced greasy boat-show food."

"I'll buy the beer."

❖

Unfortunately having the duty also meant not consuming any alcohol. Lane had three beers while Kyle nursed a Coke as they prowled the boats lined up neatly on the convention hall floor. Lane was particularly interested in a forty-foot sailboat and spent at least twenty minutes below deck surveying the quarters. She was startled at a voice close behind her.

"Are you going to memorize every detail or just take her home?"

Kyle was standing so close that her warm breath tickled Lane's ear. The heat radiating off Kyle's body intensified when she moved a fraction closer so that their bodies touched. There was no one else on the boat.

Lane consciously shifted her weight and leaned into the warm embrace. "I'm not sure yet."

Kyle pressed her crotch into the firm ass in front of her and wrapped her arms around Lane. "What do you need to decide?"

"I need to be comfortable that I can handle her. I have to know she'll respond unquestionably to my commands." Lane ran her fingers down the bare arms that encircled her waist. Kyle shivered when her nails replaced her fingertips.

Are we talking about the boat? "From what I've seen, I think she'd do anything you ask her to. Even more if you let her."

"Think so?" Lane had a difficult time concentrating as Kyle nibbled on her ear.

"Mm-hmm."

"Well, since you put it that way," Lane slid out of Kyle's embrace and headed toward the cabin door, "I think I will take her home." She took Kyle's hand and when they were topside grabbed a brochure off the table. She was seriously thinking about getting a boat and the one they just stepped off of was perfect. Lane continued to hold Kyle's hand as they walked through the thinning crowd of people and out into the cool night air. "Do you sail, Detective?"

Kyle had been concentrating on the fact that Lane was leading her in no uncertain terms back to the car and most likely into her bed. "Excuse me?"

Lane smiled. "I asked if you sailed?" *She's rattled again.*

"As in a sailboat?"

"Is there any other?"

Kyle was not a sailor by any means and she searched her mind to see if that was a real question or a continuation of the innuendo they had begun on the boat. "We are talking about a boat, aren't we?"

Lane stopped in the shadow of a tree cast by a street light and turned to Kyle. "Of course we are, silly. What else would we be talking about?" She was thrilled she could unhinge such a powerful woman.

"No I've never been on a sailboat. Have you?" Kyle commanded her head to clear.

Lane stepped closer and leaned in close to Kyle's ear. "Yes, I have and if you pick the right one she'll respond unquestionably to your commands and is soft and smooth in all the right places. That is if you can handle her." Lane punctuated her statement by moving so that their breasts were touching.

Jesus Christ, I'm so hot I don't even know what we're talking about.

Lane's voice got softer and huskier. "And I think you'd be able to handle her quite well, Detective. In your hands she'd do everything you'd want her to."

Oh shit. Kyle couldn't stop herself and she gently cupped Lane's face. "Promise? I don't have any experience in that area."

The burning desire in Lane's eyes mirrored the heat between Kyle's legs, and she slowly lowered her head until their lips were not quite brushing.

"I have every faith in your ability, Detective." Lane's voice was just above a whisper.

She gasped as Kyle's warm lips touched hers and began a gentle exploration. There was no space between them, and the heat continued to rise. Kyle's touch was tentative on her face and her tongue traced the outline of her lips.

Kyle twisted her fingers into thick, wavy hair that felt like strands of silk. She caressed Lane's back in a slow circular pattern, and when she moved her hands south, Lane moaned and stumbled backwards against a tree trunk. Kyle slipped a thigh between Lane's legs and was rewarded with another moan.

She dragged her mouth away gasping for air. *Am I going too fast?* Even if their acquaintanceship had mostly comprised casual conversation until their recent dates, it wasn't as if they were strangers.

"Touch me." Lane's throat was hoarse, and her body pounded with need. She didn't care that they were in a public place. It had been far too long since she'd been kissed like this, and her body was alive. She shivered as she felt Kyle's lips burn a trail across her face and neck as her hands slid under her shirt.

Kyle was so hot she could hardly breathe. Lane's skin was warm and quivered where her hands traveled. Her fingers brushed over lace covered nipples, and Lane inhaled sharply filling Kyle's hands with full breasts. Kneading the soft flesh, Kyle teased Lane's hard nipples, alternatively tweaking and grazing them with her thumbs. Lane's ragged breathing matched the teasing strokes.

Lane pulled her back into a fierce kiss grinding her lips against her even harder than Kyle thought imaginable. The world started spinning, and just when Kyle thought she might faint from lack of oxygen, Lane tore her mouth away.

"Touch me."

This time the command had a very different meaning, and there was no doubt in Kyle's mind what Lane was talking about. Reluctantly she pulled her hands away from Lane's breasts and slid them slowly down her tight stomach. Shaking slightly, she opened the first button on Lane's pants.

"Yes." Lane whispered in her ear, further inflaming her burning desire.

The second button was easier, and when Lane swirled her tongue around her ear, Kyle didn't even bother with the rest. She slid her hand under Lane's silky panties and soft hair tickled her palm. She was on fire, her passion quickly taking her to a place she had never been. Her mind was screaming at her to slow down and savor the moment, but her body wasn't listening. Lights flashed in her brain when Lane arched into her hand.

The instant her fingers encountered warm, wet flesh her pager went off. *Shit! Fuck! Not now!* She stilled her hands. She was on the verge of being totally out of control.

"This had damn well better be good," she mumbled breathing heavily trying to regain command of her senses.

Lane was instantly cool where she had once been blistering hot. She took a deep breath and studied the face of the first woman she had wanted to have touch her since her surgery. Sarcastically, she said, "So much for living on the edge."

"This is a little too close to the edge for me." Kyle glanced around the very public location they'd chosen for their very private activity. "I'm sorry. I've got to get this."

She started to turn away and reach for her phone. She was stopped by a trembling hand on her arm. Then, Lane softly caressed her cheek.

"It's okay," she said. "It would have been terribly embarrassing to be arrested for indecent exposure at my age." Lane smiled when the soft teasing produced the desired result—a smile from the tough detective.

Twenty minutes later Kyle was standing over a dead twenty-year-old, and Lane was standing naked in a cold shower.

❖

Lane was bent over her desk sorting through the bills that had arrived in the day's mail. *I really need to hire someone to do this.* She knew every aspect of her business, and in the beginning it was easy to handle all the administration herself; but as the restaurant grew, it became more and more difficult to keep it all straight. She never minded the paperwork side of the business, but since her surgery she found that she'd rather be spending her time with her customers than with a calculator.

Her attempts at organization were mercifully interrupted by the telephone. She immediately forgot about reconciling the accounts and picked up the receiver. She smiled at the voice on the other end. "Hello, Detective."

God it's good to hear her voice. Kyle had spent the entire night conducting the preliminary stages of the investigation of the murder of a junior at Cal State, Spencer Collins. The crime scene was ugly even by a seasoned detective's standards with blood spatter covering just about every surface of the room where Collins was discovered. His parents had bought him the condo that held his dead body. He'd been stabbed with what the coroner preliminarily identified as a large blade knife and, from the number of wounds, the attack appeared to be emotionally motivated.

"Hello yourself, Ms. Connor. How is *your* day going?" Kyle immediately felt refreshed just making small talk with this woman.

"Probably better than yours. Did you get any sleep?" *I know I didn't for an altogether different reason.*

Kyle thought about the four empty coffee cups she had left in the dumpster outside the station. "No, I just got back to my desk."

Lane felt a wave of sympathy for her. "Does this happen often?"

Kyle put her feet on her desk and rubbed her hands across her tired face. "Sometimes. The first twenty-four hours of an investigation are the most critical. The evidence is the freshest, and the witnesses haven't forgotten anything yet."

Kyle usually didn't reveal so much about her work to the women she dated. She always had the impression they were asking due to morbid curiosity, and she was not going to be used to satisfy their thirst for true crime. She didn't get that impression with Lane.

"Can I bring you anything? Some coffee or something to eat?" Lane glanced at the clock. "Oh my goodness Kyle, it's after two. Have you eaten *anything*?"

"I grabbed a bite before I came in. It certainly wasn't your cinnamon muffin, but it did take care of the hunger pangs." The muffins served at The SandPiper were the best Kyle had ever tasted.

"Okay, but if you need anything will you call me?"

"Yes. And Lane...I want to apologize again for last night. The life of a detective has its perks, but sometimes it sucks big time, and last night was one of them." Kyle had had a hard time concentrating on her crime scene as all her blood settled in her crotch at the memory of Lane's kisses.

"Perks? What kind of perks?"

"Well, the fact that I get to be called 'Detective' by a gorgeous woman. That doesn't happen to just any old cop you know."

Lane could hear the fatigue in Kyle's voice. "Well, what do you know. We have something else in common. I don't call just any old cop 'Detective.'" She liked using the professional moniker.

Kyle warmed inside. "I'll remember that." She saw her captain motion for her. "I'm sorry, I've gotta go. Can I call you tomorrow?"

"Sure, call me when you can." Lane didn't want to add any extra pressure to Kyle's already heavy burdens.

"Okay. And Lane?"

"Yes," Lane replied expectantly.

"I really enjoyed myself last night." Kyle hadn't felt this good since Alison died.

Lane smiled as she flushed with desire. "I did too. Maybe next time we'll get to go sailing."

Kyle smiled at the innuendo. "I look forward to it. I'll call you tomorrow." Kyle hung up the phone, gathered her notebook and dragged herself out of the chair.

❖

It was more like four days later when Kyle called, and she couldn't hide the weariness in her voice. "I'm sorry."

Lane's heart tugged when she heard the apology. "Kyle, you don't have to apologize." She didn't get to finish her thought.

Kyle's voice was stronger this time. "Yes, I do. I said I'd call on Thursday and today's Monday. I got tied up in this investigation and I've hardly even been home."

That was an understatement. Spencer Collins was the only son of State Senator Marcus Collins who wasted no time in throwing his considerable weight around with the Chief of Police. He demanded hourly updates of the investigation in the murder of his son, and between pacifying the Senator, the Chief and actually conducting the investigation, she had only been home to shower and change her clothes.

"I know. I saw you on the news."

Lane had been flipping through the channels when a familiar face caught her attention. Kyle was giving a statement to the media and they kept interrupting with questions. There were dark circles under her eyes, and the characteristic sharpness of her clothing was missing. During the press conference, Kyle had never lost her composure as she answered the same questions several times.

Kyle chuckled. "Yeah, not my finest hour, I'm afraid."

Usually she had the patience necessary to deal with the incessant and frequently banal questions of the reporters. Kyle was exhausted and frustrated by Senator Collins' interference in the case. They had a suspect, and she was worried that when they made an arrest, there would be a rush to justice. Senator Collins would not let up until his son's killer was convicted.

"You're too hard on yourself, Kyle." She heard a long sigh.

"Are you free for lunch tomorrow? I should be able to get away for a while." Kyle stretched her legs out on the couch and reached for the cold bottle of beer on the table next to her. She'd been home several hours, and in that time she'd used up all the hot water soaking in the tub. She had then spent the next hour playing with Hollie, and once the youngster had settled in for her morning nap, she had called Lane.

"Kyle, I don't want to interfere—"

"I want to see you Lane." Kyle's response was more forceful than she intended. She was emotionally drained and physically exhausted and had to force herself to stay awake. She softened her tone. "And I have to eat, anyway, so I'll be accomplishing two things at once."

CHAPTER EIGHT

"What's with the buckets of paint sitting by the front door?"

Lane was surprised to see Kyle walk through the door. She had expected her to call about lunch, but the sudden leap in her stomach told her that seeing Kyle in person was much better. Her pulse raced. Today Kyle was not wearing a jacket, and she envisioned the muscles that she had so closely touched a few days before beneath the blue oxford shirt. "Paint?"

Kyle smiled at Lane's obvious distraction. *She feels the way I do when I see her.* "Yes, paint. You know the stuff you put on the walls for color," Kyle said mischievously.

"I can see why they made you a detective. You're pretty sharp. I bet nothing gets by you." Lane started to walk past her to retrieve the paint. She was stopped by Kyle's warm hand on her arm.

"Does that include you?" Kyle stepped close enough that her forearm barely brushed against Lane's breasts. Her eyes seductively roamed over Lane's body while she waited for her answer. Lane felt her nipples harden at the light touch, and a jolt of passion exploded in her groin. She leaned into the hard body in front of her, knowing that Kyle was aware of her arousal. "Do you *want* me to get by you?"

"What do you think?"

Kyle gazed intently into the smoldering eyes that taunted her. She knew that with one word she could have Lane right here, right now. *Yeah, right, and she could have me right here, right now too.* She lowered her eyes to the red lips that had caressed her own so briefly just days ago. Her breath caught in her throat when Lane's tongue snaked out and unconsciously licked them.

Lane's desire was so overwhelming it took several moments for Kyle's question to sink in. Teasing lips were inches from hers, and she slid her free hand behind Kyle's neck. Closing the distance between them, she softly whispered, "I think you'd better kiss me again."

Her head exploded at the contact, and she swayed against the hard body in front of her. She forgot where she was and opened her mouth to deepen the kiss.

Kyle caught her breath as their tongues met. She reeled from the sensations coursing through her body. The feel of this woman in her arms again was so right and natural, she wanted to hold her forever. Lane grasped her neck tighter. Kyle almost fell completely into the kiss but somehow common sense fought its way to the surface. She pulled away.

"Lane, we're standing in the middle of your doorway. People are going to want to come in." Her breath was ragged and her hands trembled.

Lane couldn't have cared less where they were or who was coming in. All she knew was the exquisite feeling of being in Kyle's arms. Someone cleared their throat behind her, and she stepped away from the object of her desire, amazed her legs were still holding her up.

"Yeah, you're right. Are you always so level headed?"

Passion-filled eyes returned her gaze. "God, I hope not."

They finished their lunch quickly, and Lane answered Kyle's original question. "I'm painting the patio this weekend. The weather and the salt do a real number out here, and it's starting to look a little ragged."

Kyle looked around the outdoor seating area. Kyle's trained eye could see the places that Lane talked about. However Kyle doubted that anyone else would notice. "Did you say *you* are painting the patio?"

"Of course! I painted it the first time and the second, and I can certainly do it this time. Some of the wait staff offered to help again this year. We close it off to customers first thing Saturday morning and open it again Sunday morning."

"Would you like an extra hand?"

Lane was distracted when Kyle stretched her legs under the table. Her navy trousers pulled snugly over her thighs, accentuating the tight muscles beneath. "I'm sorry, what did you say?"

Kyle swallowed a smile, enjoying Lane's flustered glances. "I asked if you'd like an extra pair of hands. I've been known to paint a pretty straight line."

The exercise would do her good; she needed to get her mind off the stalemate in several of her cases. The only positive outcome in the past few days was the arrest of Spencer Collins's killer. Their investigation had led them to his ex-girlfriend, who folded like a house of cards five minutes into the interrogation. According to the girl, Senator Collins didn't approve of her and had demanded that his son end their relationship or he would cut off all financial support. Spencer did as he was told, and the ex was pissed and stabbed him fourteen times. The senator was not nearly as grateful as he was critical of the department's handling of his son's case. Kyle hadn't expected anything different, so she wouldn't lose any sleep. Right now, all that mattered to her was being with the woman sitting in front of her.

The thought of spending the day with Kyle in the sunshine and fresh air appealed to her. Lane didn't know what Kyle typically did on the weekends, but she suspected she valued her free time. "You don't have to do that."

"I wouldn't have asked if I didn't want to." When Lane didn't answer, Kyle prompted "Come on, what kind of damage can one woman do with a little paint. I promise, I'll clean up any mess I make." She had just about given up hope for a positive reply when Lane finally spoke.

"I can only imagine what you could do with a little paint." Lane got up from the table and Kyle followed. Lane reached up and surprised Kyle by quickly kissing her cheek. "We start at seven. Don't be late or you're on clean up duty."

❖

"Kyle, are you listening to me?"

"Of course I am."

"Then what did I just say?"

Kyle turned to the man who'd been sitting next to her in the passenger seat for the past three hours. Travis had received a reliable tip that the prime suspect in the homicide of Gloria Faulkner was staying in the nondescript house they were watching. So far the guy hadn't made an appearance, but Kyle knew he would. He'd been Gloria's pimp, and she wasn't the only girl in his stable. He would step out the door to check on his girls as he did every night, and they would be there. They could have simply knocked on the front door, but their informant had warned them that there were several guns inside. It would be safer to make their arrest on the street.

Kyle resigned herself to the fact that she'd been caught daydreaming. "I have no idea what you said."

Travis raised his eyebrows. Ordinarily Kyle was never distracted while working. In their occupation it was imperative that they remained aware of their surroundings at all times. Officers throughout the country paid the ultimate price when they didn't realize there was a gun in the back of their head until it was too late.

"Are you seeing Lane?" Travis asked.

He knew her well enough to have guessed at the reason for her wool-gathering, and he was probably tired of waiting for her to spill. Kyle didn't share much of her personal life at work, and she was aware that several detectives saw her as unfriendly.

Cagily, she stalled. "What makes you ask that?"

"You've changed," Travis said with conviction. "It's subtle and if someone didn't know you as well as I do, they wouldn't suspect a thing. Now, give it up."

"Okay, we've gone out. So what?"

"Bain, I'm in no mood to drag out every answer. Spill it or I'll sick Joann on you, and you won't come out until you've coughed up your grandmother's biscuit recipe." Travis' wife Joann was almost a better interrogator than her husband.

Kyle sighed at the inevitable. "We've gone out a couple of times, that's all."

"So far."

"Travis," she warned. It wasn't as though she hadn't thought that far ahead, but she had no plans to discuss the details with her partner.

"Come on Kyle, she's hot. If you don't sleep with her, you're definitely not a lesbian. What's stopping you? Not that you jump into bed with everybody—"

"Not *everybody*, only those who buy me dinner." They both laughed and the tension dissolved. "Seriously Travis, Lane's different. There's a connection that I haven't felt with anyone before. It's more than physical, it's almost kinetic, for lack of a better word."

"So you two are clicking pretty good?" Travis regarded her skeptically. It was both a question and a statement.

"Yeah, we are."

"Then what's the problem?" Travis made it obvious on several previous occasions that he wanted nothing more than to see his partner as happily married as he was.

"I can't, not yet."

"Why not?"

"I haven't told her about Hollie."

"You what? Jesus Christ, Kyle, she's a child, not a lifelong venereal disease!"

Kyle was frustrated with his incessant questioning of her actions. *Or lack thereof.* "You don't understand."

"No, Kyle, I don't. Enlighten me, please."

Kyle was saved from answering as a lanky man in a green fatigue jacket walked out of the house. "That's him, let's go."

❖

Lane woke early in anticipation of seeing Kyle again. She lay in bed as she had much of the night thinking about her detective. Between her friends and customers, Lane knew a lot of different women, but none were as intriguing as the one she was seeing now. Kyle was always so in control. There were times when she thought Kyle was about to let her in, but then suddenly she would pull back. Kyle was funny, knew the oddest trivial facts, was definitely attractive, and she oozed confidence but wasn't cocky. She was always aware of her surroundings, but never appeared nosey. She saw ugliness every day but didn't have a trace of bitterness. She was genuinely polite and treated Lane like she was the most important woman in the world. All of that in a stunningly wrapped package was the icing on the cake. *And holy cow what a kisser!*

She touched her lips remembering Kyle's first kiss. The soft tentative exploration was more like a request for permission to kiss, versus taking possession. Each time Kyle touched her or kissed her it was the same. She was finally able to put her finger on what was so different. Kyle respected her, and Lane had not felt that from a woman in a long time.

She slid out of bed smiling this time at the butterflies dancing around in her stomach. She was going to see Kyle today, and she couldn't wait. She hurried into the shower, shaved her legs all the way up and brushed her teeth twice as long as usual. She laughed while she ironed an old pair of cut-off jeans, but she wouldn't dream of letting Kyle see her a wrinkled mess. As she drove to The SandPiper she felt like she was teetering on the edge of something she desperately wanted to step over.

Thirty minutes later, Lane turned into the lot, parking her car in the space next to the sleek Saab convertible. Kyle could not stop her eyes from traveling up and down Lane's long legs as she stepped out of the car. Lane's shorts were shorter than she wore while working, and if the increased speed of her pulse was any indication, Kyle predicted it was going to be a very interesting day.

"Good morning," Lane said. "You're here early."

Kyle was waiting by the front door of The SandPiper and approached Lane's car when she pulled into the parking space. "Well, you know, the early bird gets the best paint brush." Kyle could barely restrain a grin.

"And gets to make the coffee." Lane handed her a box of bagels then grasped Kyle's T-shirt by the neck and pulled her in for a quick kiss. Lane winked at Kyle's surprise and quickly unlocked the front door of The SandPiper.

It wasn't long before tables and chairs were moved, the tarps put down, and the painting begun. Eight of Lane's staff were making good progress on the east side of the patio while Lane and Kyle attacked the trim. They broke for lunch, but not before Kyle had been caught staring at Lane's legs several times. One of those times, as she'd handed a rag to Lane, her face had been inches from the back of Lane's knee. She was an instant away from running her tongue over the smooth surface when they were interrupted by one of the busboys asking for more paint. Kyle had recoiled so fast, she almost tripped over her paint tray.

After lunch, the sun beat down on the patio, and Lane handed out bottles of water so her workers were properly hydrated. She rounded the corner where Kyle was working and found her three steps up on a ladder. Kyle didn't notice her at first, which gave her an uninterrupted opportunity to observe her favorite helper. She stared at the paint spattered running shoes and the legs that had obviously been used for running miles and miles. The hard muscles in Kyle's calves tensed when she stood on her toes to reach a spot just out of her reach. The reach also provided Lane a glimpse all the way up the back of a firm thigh. She didn't see any sign of a panty line but then again she didn't think Kyle was the type to wear conventional underwear. *I'll bet she wears boxers.*

Licking her lips at the thought, she watched the muscles in Kyle's arms flex as she raised the paint brush over her head. A light sheen of sweat covered the tan skin exposed by the cut off sleeves of the La Jolla PD T-shirt. If she were just a step closer, she would be able to peek under the cut off bottom of the shirt. Her curiosity got the best of her and she did just that. *Oh my!*

She stopped breathing at the sight of a stomach hard and tanned all the way up to the white band of a sports bra. Taking full advantage of her position, she openly devoured the area with her eyes. The flesh was irresistible. Lane totally forgot where they were, and before she knew what was happening, she'd reached out to touch the warm skin.

Kyle had sensed that someone was behind her, and when they didn't say anything, she knew it could only be one person. She chose not to let Lane know that she was aware of her, opting instead to see what she would do. The longer Lane watched her, the more difficult it was for her not to let on. Her body burned as if Lane was actually touching her. She heard Lane move and was prepared for her touch. What she wasn't prepared for was the explosion that ignited in her stomach right under Lane's fingers. Somehow she managed to act not surprised. She turned her head and looked under her arm.

"What are you doing?" Her voice cracked under the strain of maintaining control.

Lane quickly dropped her hand and stepped back, embarrassed. *Wait, I have nothing to be embarrassed about.*

"What do you think I'm doing?" she asked. She enjoyed toying with the tough detective.

Kyle didn't move. "Making me crazy."

Lane's eyes sparkled with a combination of desire and mischief. "Really?"

Kyle stepped down one step. "I think," she stepped down another, "that you," she went down the final step and her body brushed against Lane's, "know exactly what you're doing."

That was not the response Lane expected, but she was thrilled nonetheless. Kyle didn't move any closer. Her eyes were pinpoints of desire and, staring into them, Lane could feel her chest rising and falling with small shudders. Her breathing grew shallow. Her hands itched to touch the wavy dark hair blowing in the wind. She had never felt so wound up from the closeness of a woman. The tension between them increased as the silence stretched unbearably. Not sure if she wanted it to continue or be released from it, she took a step forward, letting her breasts come into contact with Kyle's.

"Does it bother you?" she asked innocently.

Kyle breathed deeper and her eyes flared with desire. "What bothers me is that there are eight people too many here to allow you to finish what you've started."

Before Lane had a chance to reply, two of those people called for her from the other side of the deck. An interruption was the last thing she wanted at his very moment. Struggling to control her breathing, she cursed, "Fuck!"

"No thanks, not right now." Kyle kissed Lane quickly on the lips. "Maybe later though." She raised her eyebrows.

Lane's face was flushed with passion, and she licked her lips in unconscious anticipation. Kyle yearned to do something about her transparent need, but this was not the time or place. Besides, the wait would keep them both on edge, and she enjoyed making love under those circumstances. Holding that thought and resisting the silent plea in Lane's expression, she went back up the ladder.

❖

Several hours later the patio sported a fresh coat of paint, the mess was cleaned up, the workers fed, and they were all sharing a washtub of ice cold beer. The guys were playing a game of touch football while Lane and Kyle sat in the sand, their backs against the seawall that protected the patio from the tidal surge.

Kyle dangled her long-neck beer from hands that rested on top of her bent knees. The sun had just touched the water and for the first time in days she felt totally relaxed. She'd been struggling with her feelings for Lane and couldn't quite put her finger on what was so different about how she felt when they were together. The best way she could describe it was that she felt at peace.

Lane watched the sun hit the water and reflected on her day spent with the enigmatic woman sitting next to her. Her heart had been racing ever since she saw Kyle first thing this morning and could not return to its normal rate while she sat this close. Her skin tingled where she remembered Kyle touching her, and her body craved more. She felt the heat emanating from Kyle's body and desperately wanted to be wrapped in its warm cocoon. Kyle's voice interrupted her thoughts.

"It felt good to get out and do something physical all day. I've been buried under mounds of paperwork." She finished her beer and reached for another.

Lane could stand it no longer. "It felt good touching you." Her voice was so quiet she wasn't sure if Kyle heard her, but judging by her reaction, she had.

Kyle's hand froze on the bottle cap. "Yes, it did, very good."

They stared at each other, their eyes doing all the talking.

Shaken by what she saw, Lane finally asked, "So, what do we do now?"

"We find some privacy. Let's walk."

Lane accepted Kyle's outstretched hand and got to her feet. Kyle didn't let go of her hand but held it firmly as they started walking. After several minutes, they were far enough from the people that the sound of the lapping water was all they heard. The night was cool and the occasional spray of sea water crashing over rocks was invigorating. Kyle seemed to be lost in her thoughts, and Lane didn't know what to say, if anything so she said nothing at all. A fog horn sounded in the distance.

"Lane, there's something I have to tell you."

Oh shit, she's already in a relationship. Lane's step faltered.

Kyle saw Lane's reaction and quickly said, "No, no, it's

not bad. I'm not married or dying or anything like that. I have a daughter. She's a year old, and my sister's child. Alison died shortly after Hollie was born."

"You have a daughter? Kyle, that's wonderful. Tell me about her. Do you have a picture? Is she walking yet?" She was full of questions and couldn't remember when she'd felt more relieved.

Kyle reached into her wallet, and Lane saw that her hand was shaking. She grasped the shaking hand with one of her own. "Kyle, it's all right." The sky was clear, providing enough light for Lane to see the photo. "My God. She looks just like you."

Kyle chuckled. "She should. Alison and I were identical twins."

Lane's hand flew to her mouth masking a gasp. Just as quickly she lowered it and took Kyle's hand. "I'm sorry."

The simple words meant a lot. "Thanks. It's been quite a transition for both of us. I certainly wasn't prepared to raise a child, and Hollie didn't expect to be raised by someone other than her mother. But we're getting along pretty good."

"Who watches her when you're at work?" Lane thought about the times they had gone out and today. "Kyle, you've been here all day. Where is she now?"

"My parents have her for the weekend. I also have a nanny. Gretchen has been with me since Hollie came home. I have a guest house that she lives in, which makes it convenient when I have to work late or I'm called in. Hollie adores her and I'm grateful to have her."

"That's right, you said your parents live close, didn't you?"

"Yes, they live over on Invergordon. They see Hollie all the time. Sometimes I think they see her more than I do." Like any other working mother, Kyle struggled to balance the demands of a job she loved with her need to parent a child she loved even more.

Lane hesitated before asking her next question, not sure if she wanted to hear the answer. "Why did you wait so long to tell me?" She wasn't mad but couldn't fathom why Kyle hadn't told her earlier.

"I wanted to be a little more sure of us. That we got along, had fun and...you know." Kyle felt foolish that she had waited. "Most women don't want an instant family, especially one with baggage like this."

Hollie would always be a constant reminder of Alison. Kyle would never get over the death of her sister, but she was learning how to move on. She had to, for Hollie's sake.

"You were afraid I would lose interest because you have a child?" Lane's question was not accusatory, but she looked directly into Kyle's eyes for the answer.

"I want to be careful who I bring into Hollie's life," Kyle said. "I don't want women parading in and out of our home. I don't want Hollie forming attachments when there's nothing... secure."

"Do you see me as part of that *parade*?"

Kyle grasped Lane's hands. "Absolutely not. That's not what I meant. What I mean is that my life is different now that I have a child. Everything I do affects her in some way. And I'm going to do my damnedest to make sure it's positive."

Lane read the love of her child in Kyle's expression, and she wanted to meet the little girl who looked so much like the woman standing in the moonlight. Her heart ached at the uncertainty on Kyle's face. She knew of one way to change that and wrapped her arms around Kyle's neck. "I'm glad you told me." Drawing Kyle to her, she kissed her.

Kyle walked Lane to her car and made another major decision. "There's another reason why I had to tell you about Hollie."

Lane stopped as she unlocked the door. "And that is?"

Kyle gently cupped Lane's cheek in her hand while she ran her thumb over red lips. Her eyes blazed a trail across the smooth face, and she was certain her desire was written all over her own face. "I want to make love with you, and I couldn't until I told you. That would've been wrong and deceitful."

Lane appreciated the risk Kyle had taken with the revelation that she had a child. She very easily could have walked away, and she was sure many women would. Another element of Kyle's character was standing exposed in front of her. To Kyle, omission of the information would be just as bad as an outright lie.

Lane drank in the desire Kyle made no attempt to hide. Her heart beat faster. "Then I think you'd better follow me home."

Chapter Nine

K yle's nerves jumped when Lane closed the door behind her. *This woman is special and I don't want to screw this up.*

Lane's hand shook as she set her keys on the table. "So Hollie is with your parents tonight?"

Kyle appreciated her checking in about the arrangements. "Yes, she spends the night with them several times a month. Mom and Dad get to spoil her rotten, and she gets to be the center of their attention. It works out all the way around."

"And you get the night off from being Mommy as well. I imagine you need that once in a while." Lane stepped closer and wrapped her hands around Kyle's arm leading her over to the couch. "You know, I have something you need to know as well. Something that's next to impossible to hide even if I wanted to, which I don't."

Kyle took both of Lane's hands in hers but said nothing. She had been in enough difficult conversations to recognize this was going to be one of them and searched for a reason. Suddenly, it dawned on her, and she felt her heart catapult into her throat. Lane had been intentionally vague with the details about her illness, and Kyle was terrified that she was sicker than she let on. Memories of the pain she endured when Alison died engulfed her like a shroud.

"When I was sick last year, I had heart surgery. They had to go in and do some tinkering, but everything is fine now. I have a scar that runs from here to here." She pulled her hands from Kyle's to indicate the length of the scar on her chest.

Jesus I had no idea. "Are you self-conscious about it?" Relief flooded over her as Lane explained.

"No. But you're the first one to see it."

Kyle understood the meaning of Lane's words and felt honored. The adrenaline caused by fear was quickly replaced with desire. "You are exquisite." Then she kissed her.

Lane's lips were as soft as she remembered, and she felt the familiar jolt of electricity at the connection. Lane grasped her hair and pulled her closer as their kiss exploded in passion. She gently pushed Lane back on the couch and covered her body with her own never breaking the kiss. Kyle's hands couldn't be still. She found the buttons on Lane's shirt. As she unfastened them, she felt Lane's lips move down her neck.

Lane was not about to let Kyle have all the action. She pulled Kyle's shirt from her shorts and felt the sharp intake of breath as her hands met skin that burned with desire. She moaned in pleasure as she caressed the muscles in Kyle's strong back.

Kyle shifted on the couch to make more room. Her head spun when she opened Lane's shirt to expose the skin beneath. A lacy, cobalt blue bra encased the perfectly formed breasts that had invaded her dreams. Lane's smooth, creamy skin and her erect nipples called out to Kyle. The scar was a pale red line that did nothing to detract from the beauty facing her now.

"You are so beautiful." Kyle whispered. She couldn't wait and reached for the bra. It opened in the front. *Whoever invented these is a saint.*

Full breasts spilled out of their enclosure and into Kyle's trembling hands. She caressed each one with her eyes, and her mouth watered in anticipation. When her lips met the delicate skin, Lane moaned and urged her closer. She feasted on one breast not quite circling the rosy nipple that was straining for her attention.

Oh my god. This feels wonderful. Lane squirmed with desire, and her nerves screamed out for Kyle to take her nipple between her teeth. Kyle must have read her mind as a rocket of desire shot through Lane's body when she felt warm lips close over her puckered flesh.

"Oh, God. Kyle, that feels wonderful."

Kyle reacted by applying the same amount of attention to the adjoining breast. She took her time wanting to savor every sensation, and starting on the outer edges of Lane's breast, slowly licked and kissed every inch of the warm flesh. Finally, when she could wait no longer, she captured Lane's thrusting nipple between her teeth. Lane dug her fingers into her hair and pulled her closer. Torn between her desire to stay right where she was and the pulsing in her crotch, she dragged her mouth from the breasts and kissed a trail up Lane's neck.

"Is there a bedroom somewhere near by?" she asked with difficulty. Her mouth felt a little swollen, and her throat was tight and dry.

Lane laughed and sat up, pulling Kyle with her. "This way."

She was surprised that her legs were able to support her as she led Kyle down the hall. She hadn't made love since weeks before her surgery, and she was shaking with desire. She led Kyle into her bedroom and turned to her. Their eyes met, and she was stunned at the raging passion deep within. She closed the distance and her pent up passion burst to the surface. She dragged Kyle's shirt over her head and tossed it somewhere behind her. The muscles hidden underneath the smooth tanned skin were hard and defined to her touch. She reached for the snap on Kyle's shorts. She felt Kyle shudder at the contact.

Lane chuckled as she released the snap and slid the zipper down, her fingers tracing the path settling tightly against the fabric where it came to a halt. Kyle grabbed her wrist and stopped her descent even further. Her voice was laced with passion as her lips traversed the expanse of bare flesh on Lane's chest.

Between kisses and soft bites, she said, "Wait. I want you so bad I might come right here and now if you keep that up. And that's not what I want to do."

Lane's knees buckled at Kyle's comment on the state of arousal. Somehow she found her voice. "And what is it you *would* like to do Detective?"

Lane soon found out.

Their lovemaking was slow and intense. Kyle gently lowered her onto the bed touching the soft, silky skin exposed as she removed the remainder of Lane's clothes. She explored Lane's body with her hands and when she replaced her hands with her lips, Lane called out her name.

It's been so long since I've felt another woman's hands on me. God it feels wonderful. Lane felt more alive than ever before. Whether it was because of her heightened sense of life after her surgery, or because of the woman that was touching her, she wasn't certain. When Kyle nibbled on a particularly sensitive spot, Lane knew it was definitely the woman. The more Kyle stroked and caressed her, the more aroused she became until she began to lose herself, switching off everything but the magic of Kyle's skin against hers and the ache building at her core.

Kyle had always wanted to give the woman she was with as much sexual pleasure as she was receiving, but making love with Lane was different. Lane's body clearly and unabashedly responded to her touch, and Kyle was solely intent on giving her immeasurable pleasure. She couldn't recall such single-mindedness with a woman before, and she stopped thinking about it and simply enjoyed her.

She blazed a trail up and down Lane's body, resisting the temptation to go immediately to Lane's core. She needed to touch her, to feel her. Their encounter after the boat show was an agonizing memory of what almost was. Lane must have remembered it as well, thrusting her hips in Kyle's direction whenever she got close. With deliberate slowness, she kissed Lane, and her fingers gently entered the warm folds that had beckoned her for so long. Lane moaned against her lips and pulled her tighter.

Kyle showered kisses on Lane's face and neck as she slowly explored the warm, wet area with her fingers. She felt Lane's hands travel over her back. Her grip intensified when Kyle found a particularly sensitive spot. She sensed Lane was on the brink of orgasm several times and gently altered the intensity of her touch just enough to delay the inevitable.

"Jesus, you're killing me." Lane moaned as her body once again crawled back from climax.

"No, I'm not. I'm enjoying you." Kyle descended her body with a succession of kisses and came precariously close to the warm heat that she had recently caressed with her fingers. "You're a strong girl, I think you can handle it."

Somehow Lane managed a coherent thought. "But what if I don't want to be strong?" *I'm so weak from desire right now I couldn't possibly.* "What if I just want…"

She gasped and her voice trailed off as Kyle's lips found her clitoris and began doing wonderful things to it. Kyle almost came as Lane's body reacted to her tongue. She focused her attention away from her own throbbing clit and onto that of the woman whose juices flowed freely from her. *God, you are magnificent.*

Kyle had made love to numerous women, but none had made her feel this way; without restraint and yet protective at the same time.

"What do you want?" Kyle asked as she slipped one finger into the dripping opening. She squeezed her thighs together tightly as she willed herself not to come. *Oh god, I shouldn't have done that.*

Lane's breaths were coming in short staccato gasps. The feel of Kyle's mouth on her clit, and her fingers inside her was unbearable. "I...want...to...come," and on the last word she did.

Stars exploded behind her eyes, and she closed them to experience the most intense orgasm she had ever had. Wave after wave of passion rolled through her body and exploded under Kyle's masterful tongue. Just when she thought she had crested for the last time, Kyle shifted her mouth, moved her fingers and made her come again. But this time she was not alone.

Jesus, you are so incredibly beautiful. Watching Lane succumb to her desire, Kyle had no choice but to abandon her self-control and ride the tide with her. Their bodies trembled in unison as Kyle watched her lover be overcome with passion. Kyle's body settled first, and as her mind cleared, she stroked Lane with her tongue and light kisses. Lane's hand touched her head, resting limply.

"Wait. I need to catch my breath."

Lane remembered her last visit to her cardiologist, when he told her she could resume all normal activities including sex. He embarrassingly cautioned her that if she felt anything out of the ordinary that she should immediately stop and call him. She chuckled when she realized that there was no way she could have stopped anything even if she wanted to.

"What's so amusing?" Kyle relaxed on Lane's thigh, her hand covering the warm wet area that kept drawing her attention.

Lane looked down her flushed body to the woman who had given her such pleasure. "My cardiologist told me that if I felt anything out of the ordinary when I was making love, I was supposed to stop and call him immediately."

Kyle smiled warmly. "Since you didn't make me stop, does this mean that you didn't feel anything out of the ordinary?"

Lane reached down and pulled Kyle into her arms and kissed her. She felt Kyle's hard nipples on her chest. "Oh I definitely felt something out of the ordinary. Several times as a matter of fact."

"Do you need to call him?"

Lane rolled Kyle onto her back.

Lane's voice was muffled by her exploration of Kyle's neck as she replied. "No. What I need to do is make love to you."

Kyle gasped as Lane found a ticklish spot below her right earlobe. "Well don't let me keep you."

She thoroughly appreciated Kyle's reply.

Somehow Kyle had shed the rest of her clothes, and Lane had no idea when. Reveling in her complete access to the woman in her bed, she mirrored the actions that Kyle had taken earlier but with her own personal touch. She nipped and bit the smooth tanned skin, quickly following up with soft, healing kisses. She memorized the taste of her skin and the smell of her body as Kyle's passion increased. She turned Kyle onto her stomach and repeated the same attention on her back spending an extraordinarily amount of time on the cleft just above the firm derriere that was thrusting against her.

She slipped her hand down the crack of Kyle's ass and entered her. *Oh my God!* Lane almost came at the wetness she encountered and the moan of pleasure that escaped from Kyle. She felt Kyle's body tense under hers. "Not yet Detective, that's an order."

Jesus, Mary, and Joseph. How am I supposed to do that? Kyle gathered the remaining strength she could muster and obeyed the order. "Yes ma'am."

Lane smiled knowing how much concentration was required from Kyle to control herself. *Jeez, I'm not sure I could do it.* And with that thought she slid her other hand under Kyle's thrusting hips and found her clitoris.

Holy shit, that did it! Somehow Kyle managed to regain control even though her mind mirrored her body and turned to mush. All she could do was feel the touch of Lane's fingers inside her as she simultaneously flicked her clit.

"Lane…"

Lane could continue this torment for hours, but she sensed Kyle was at the point of no return and let her go with one word whispered in her ear. "Now."

Kyle was trained to obey commands and eagerly followed this one. She arched her hips off the bed and let out a loud cry as she was rocked by her orgasm. Through the haze she heard soft gentle words in her ear encouraging her on. She willingly complied. After several minutes, her heart began to regain its normal beat and her breathing no longer came in gasps. She moaned her disappointment when Lane removed her fingers but was quickly rewarded with the feel of her straddling her butt. It wasn't long before Lane was riding her ass with her wet juices gliding along her path. In a few short minutes she hesitated, shuddered and fell against Kyle completely spent.

❖

Kyle woke unaccustomed to warmth along her back and warm breath on her neck. *Lane.* One word summed up both her location and her situation. And what a pleasant situation it was.

She lay quietly so as not to disturb Lane, who had snuggled up against her sometime during the night. The sun peeked through the split in the curtains and from the intensity of the rays, Kyle concluded it must be early morning. She could have stayed in this position all day, but her bladder had other priorities.

Lane shifted as she climbed out of the bed. "Sssh, go back to sleep, I'll be right back." Kyle hurried into the bathroom and quietly closed the door behind her. She looked at the woman staring back at her in the mirror. Her hair was tousled, her lips were full and slightly bruised from their kisses, and she had a suspicious red mark on her left breast. *You certainly look like you've made love all night.* Kyle smirked in the mirror as she recalled the events of the past ten hours. *Oh, yeah, you definitely fucked all night.*

Lane woke as Kyle crawled back into bed. She smelled of toothpaste, sunshine and sex. *Oh God, definitely sex. Mind blowing, totally awesome sex.* She snuggled into Kyle as soon as she lay down and. Kyle's arms immediately encased her in their warmth.

"Good morning," she said and felt Kyle smile and hold her tighter.

"Yes, it definitely is. I hope you don't mind, I used some of your toothpaste." Nothing bothered Kyle more than fuzzy teeth first thing in the morning.

"After what we did last night, you certainly could have used my toothbrush as well."

Lane's fingers started drifting across the flat, tanned stomach. Kyle's muscles twitched in response. Kyle kissed the top of the blond hair that was tickling her nose. "Well, I didn't want to be presumptuous and wear out my welcome." Lane shifted so that she was lying full length on top of Kyle. It had been far too long since she had a woman in her bed, and she was in no hurry for her to leave. She started nibbling on the lips that had driven her crazy with desire throughout the night. "It would take more than using my toothbrush for me to kick you out. As a matter of fact, I just might keep you here all day."

Kyle cupped the face that had hovered over her several times last night. Her desire was mirrored in Lane's eyes. "Promises, promises."

Lane's kisses traveled from her lips to her neck and regions south. Kyle gasped as a nipple was captured by a warm mouth, and she lifted her leg as Lane's hand drifted close. "Oh my, what a wonderful way to wake up." She was close to purring with contentment. She felt Lane smile against her stomach.

"Better than coffee at your favorite restaurant?"

"Something tells me I'll get to have this *and* my favorite coffee. I...am...one...lucky...woman." Kyle had difficulty finishing her sentence with Lane's mouth wandering around her clitoris. She was rapidly losing her train of thought.

Lane's tongue connected with the sensitive tissue, and Kyle gasped at the sensation. Lane had been in this exact same place several times during the night and had quickly learned what drove Kyle to the brink of orgasm. She was torn between wanting to savor the sights, sounds and smells of this woman and wanting to actually bring her to orgasm. Not having the strength to deny either herself or Kyle the experience, she compromised and spent just a few minutes longer than either one of them could stand before flicking her tongue over the exposed flesh. Kyle responded immediately and came hard and fast. Kyle thought she'd lost consciousness as the room swam back into focus. The first thing she noticed was the blades of the ceiling fan rotating with the beat of her heart. The second was the sound of the birds chirping. But the absolute best thing was the soft hands caressing her stomach and thighs in slow circular patterns, revitalizing her libido again.

"I repeat myself, what a wonderful way to wake up." Kyle looked down to the owner of the hands. "Come up here."

Lane smiled "I kind of like it right where I am."

"Well, I *really* like you there too, but right now I want you up here." Kyle patted her chest to indicate where she wanted Lane. Lane didn't move. "What if I promise you can go back there anytime you want to?" With that, Lane almost flew up to lie face to face with her.

"Okay, I'm here. Now can I go back down there?" Lane reached down and tangled her fingers in the damp curly hair.

Oh, I'm going to like this girl. Kyle laughed and pushed Lane onto her back. "Not yet."

❖

Two hours later, Kyle was still kissing Lane, but this time they were standing by the front door. Their hair was wet from the shower they shared after Kyle regretfully said she needed to get home. The fact that she'd made the statement forty-five minutes earlier was a testament to their desire for each other, and the amount of hot water available in Lane's house.

Kyle dragged her mouth from the lips that had kissed every inch of her body. "I never thought I'd say this, but stop, please." She gazed down the front of the open robe and her hands shook as she pulled the two pieces together. "I can't leave when you kiss me like that, and when you're dressed like this."

Lane chuckled, running her thumb over Kyle's bottom lip.

Kyle softly grabbed the tantalizing hand and held it to her heaving chest. "Stop, you're killing me."

"If I did, would an equally sensuously attractive detective interrogate me?"

Kyle growled. "No, you'd probably get Detective Buckner

and let me assure you he's no Adonis. His belly precedes him to every crime scene."

Lane relented and took a step back. "Okay, I'll take pity on you, but only because you have to go home and be a mommy. I don't want your mind distracted from your active toddler. Someone could get hurt."

This woman is something else. Not only does she make me scream with desire, but she isn't threatened by Hollie. Kyle grinned. "Lane, something tells me you'll *never* take pity on me."

Lane retraced her step and slid sensuously up the firm body that was now pinned against her front door. "Detective, you'd be amazed at what I can do to you."

Oh Christ!

Before Kyle could reply, Lane kissed her firmly yet briefly, and pushed her out the door.

Kyle faced the solid door not quite sure what had just happened. Her mind reeled from the feel of Lane's body pressed up against hers, and she kept repeating Lane's words, not quite able to believe what she'd heard. Tentatively, she knocked on the door.

"Lane?"

"Yes?" The muffled reply came instantly.

"Was that a threat or an invitation?"

Kyle heard laughter on the other side of the door.

"You're the detective," Lane said. "You figure it out."

CHAPTER TEN

The sun was brighter, the air cleaner and the traffic lighter than Kyle had seen it in many months. *Jesus, any minute I'll be breaking into a Carpenter's song.* Her mind drifted as she drove the familiar streets home. She was mature enough to categorize her feelings about last night, but they were still a little unsettling. *So where exactly do I categorize the best, mind blowing, physically satisfying, and emotionally connected sex I've ever experienced? Does it go under sex? Lust? Fucking?*

Her panties soaked again as the image of Lane in her arms invaded her brain. She had been with many lovers but had connected with none as she had with Lane. As she pulled into the drive, she thought that even though she had known Lane for a few years, she really didn't know her at all.

She had just closed the garage door when she heard the sound of car doors closing in her driveway. *Shit.* She wanted to change her clothes, and she would have preferred a long soak in the tub, but she had to settle for a fresh smile for her daughter returning home.

"Mama!" Hollie squealed as she toddled on shaky legs toward her. She was dressed in a yellow sundress and matching sandals with her dark hair secured out of her face by a banana barrette.

Kyle knelt down to catch her on the run. "There's my big girl. Where have you been?" She smiled as her daughter pointed to her mother and father coming up the sidewalk. "Did you go night-night at Grandma's house?"

Kyle was rewarded with a nodding head and two warm arms wrapped around her neck. As her parents approached, she hoped she looked normal. They'd always been able to read that *I've done something* look on her face especially if she was thrilled and excited by her deed. And the previous evening's events definitely qualified. She even felt just a little bit naughty for almost being late due to her insatiable desire for Lane. It was too new to put it all into perspective, let alone talk about it and certainly not with her parents, at least not right away.

"Hi Mom, hey Dad. Come on in." Kyle turned quickly to escape her mother's critical eye.

Hollie clamored to be put down as soon as she entered the house. She ran to her bedroom, as she always did when she arrived home from a night away, eager to play once more with her favorite toys. Kyle took the diaper bag from her mother and set it on the washer in the laundry room.

"Can I get you something to drink?" She was parched. *Must be from all that heavy breathing.* She felt a faint blush rise on her face.

Her mother fixed her with an intent stare. "No thanks, nothing for me. We just had breakfast." Sounding almost too casual, she added, "At The SandPiper."

Kyle hesitated for a split second. "Really?"

"Yes, I looked for the owner, Lane isn't it?" Constance was all innocence.

Kyle flushed again and nodded. "That's right." When she had dropped Hollie off Saturday morning, she had mentioned that she would be spending the day at The SandPiper painting.

"Well, we didn't see her. She must have had other plans this morning."

"That's not what you said earlier," Kyle's dad said.

His wife cast him a scathing look. Kyle knew something was up, and she wasn't sure she liked it.

She mimicked her father. "Yes, Constance, what *did* you say?"

Her mom shrugged. "Oh, for Pete's sake, Constance. Kyle's a grown woman. We know she dates, and occasionally I can even bring myself to admit that my daughter actually has—"

The rest of his sentence was cut off by simultaneous shrieks from the women in his life. Kyle figured from her father's laughter that they must have had priceless looks on their faces.

"You two are something else." Michael Bain said. "*You*," he looked at his wife, "told me the owner of The SandPiper was interested in our daughter." He turned toward Kyle. "And *you* have wet hair, and you're wearing the same clothes as you were yesterday. I may be a sixty-eight-year-old white guy, but I can still put two and two together."

Kyle didn't know if she was surprised by her father's observation or the fact that he had come right out with his conjecture. He wasn't done, either. "What your mother actually said was that she hoped you and Lane had a good time last night. I would venture to say that you did. Now, Connie, can we get going? As much as I love this topic, there's a game I want to watch that starts in half an hour."

Kyle couldn't believe she was standing here having a conversation about her love life with her parents. Now that she thought about it, she realized that her father had always been direct and this was no exception.

"I did have a good time," she said, trying to sound as if she were quite at ease. "Thank you for asking. However I'm a bit embarrassed that you caught me at it."

"It's not the first time."

"I was in high school that time," Kyle objected.

Her father never let her forget that incident. He'd walked in on her kissing a girl in the basement. They'd both been scared to death that he would tell the other girl's father, but all he did was calmly ask them to lock the door next time.

"Keep it up. You look great," her father said approvingly.

"Thanks Dad." No other response was necessary.

❖

Lane was late for lunch with Christina. As usual, her best friend had somehow managed to find a parking space in front of the restaurant for her new Mercedes. Lane hurried inside and sat down.

"Sorry I'm late." She sipped the iced tea that Christina had ordered for her.

"Oversleep?"

"Didn't sleep at all and didn't want to get out of bed even more." She waited for Christina to process the information.

The waitress took their order and left them alone. "Is there a hidden meaning I should be aware of? Or did you have insomnia?" Christina concentrated on Lane's face searching for her answer. She found it. "You slept with someone didn't you? You go, girl! Who was it? Do I know her? How was it? How do you feel? How's your heart?"

Lane held her hand up. "Whoa, whoa, whoa. For heaven's sake, take a breath will you?"

"Sorry, I'm just so happy for you. I've been wondering when you were going to take the plunge. I can't even imagine how hard it must have been for you with Maria leaving and the transplant."

"I know, and I appreciate the concern. You're the best friend a girl could ever have, you know that?"

Christina nodded impatiently. "Is she hot?"

"Always so sensitive. I'm touched."

"Someone had to ask," Christina said without remorse.

"Her name is Kyle Bain, and she's a detective with the La Jolla P.D. She's been coming into the restaurant almost since we opened, and after I came back to work we started talking."

"You started flirting," Christina interpreted smugly.

"True," Lane conceded. "I always knew she was interested in me but she never did anything inappropriate while Maria and I were together."

"But now that everything's changed," Christina mused, "all bets are off."

"I told her that Maria was gone. And she asked me out."

"And one thing lead to another, and you slept with her?" Christina had a one track mind.

"Not right away. We've been seeing each other for a few weeks."

"What did she say about your transplant?" Christina knew Lane didn't want to be treated any different because of her surgery.

"I didn't tell her all the details." *Here it comes…*

Christina dropped her fork. "You didn't tell her? What did you do, fuck with your clothes on? If she's a detective it's obvious that she's pretty sharp and certainly not blind."

Christina had seen Lane's scar and knew there was no way to hide it, even in the dark.

"I told her I'd had some surgery on my heart but that everything was okay now." Lane knew what was coming next.

"Kind of chicken shit wouldn't you say?"

"Christina."

"Don't Christina me. What if you'd had complications, or

even worse a heart attack? You would have scarred the woman for life, no pun intended."

"My cardiologist says I'm perfectly healthy, and I have no restrictions on my activities, and that includes sex. I feel fine. Actually, I feel fabulous."

She did feel great, never more alive in her life. When Kyle touched her, fireworks exploded in every one of her senses. When she climaxed it was as if they were one. She blushed as she tried to remember just exactly how many times that was. *Too many to count and too few to live on.*

"You do look great," Christina admitted. For months she'd been telling Lane she needed to get out more so she'd have that healthy glow once again. "But you are going to tell her, aren't you?"

The question was one Lane constantly thought about. Kyle's initial reaction to seeing the scar boded well. She wasn't appalled; she seemed to accept it like an appendectomy. Lane wondered how she would react if she knew the entire story. Would she be morbidly curious, would she pull away or be afraid to touch her? All those scenarios had passed through Lane's mind during her recovery period, when she was trying to imagine how she would get her life back together. Now, as she spent more time with Kyle, she still worried every now and then. But she felt reassured that her scar, at least, was not an issue.

"I'll tell her as soon as the time is right," Lane answered hesitantly, refusing to make eye contact with her best friend.

"Don't leave it too long." For a spoiled rich girl, Christina was very astute and totally committed to her friends.

"I won't." Lane sounded more truthful than she felt.

The two women talked for over an hour after finishing their lunch, catching up on their lives and mutual friends. As they exited the café Christina asked the question that Lane had asked herself several times. *When are you going to see her again?*

❖

Lane's phone was ringing when she opened the door. She tripped over her sandals on the way to the phone and almost fell. "Shit. Uh, hello?"

A familiar voice ran through her veins like warm water. "Lane? Are you okay? Did I call at a bad time?"

"No, I'm fine. I just tripped over my shoes and stubbed my toe as I came in. I guess that wasn't the most polite way to answer the telephone." Lane tossed the offending footwear across the room.

"Should I call back later, once you've had a chance to get settled?" Hollie had just gone down for her afternoon nap and Kyle had at least ninety minutes of peace and quiet before her life was not hers again.

"No, it's fine really. How was Hollie after her night away?"

Hmm, the first thing she asked about was Hollie. "She always has fun with Mom and Dad. They were right on my heels as I pulled in the driveway. My dad commented on the fact that I had on the same clothes that I did when I dropped Hollie off."

"He did what?"

"He also noticed my hair was still wet." Kyle still could not believe the conversation they'd had earlier that morning.

"What did you say?"

"There wasn't much I could say. My parents are pretty sharp, and the evidence was pretty clear."

"Oh, God, I'm sorry. Was it really awkward?" Kyle had talked a lot about her parents and Lane didn't think they would be angry or upset about the two of them together.

"No, actually Dad reminded me of the time he walked in on

me with a girl in high school. *That* was embarrassing. This was, I don't know, affirming."

"Affirming?"

"Yeah, he winked at me and basically said I should get laid more."

I'm going to die of embarrassment if I ever meet these people. "Ugh. I would have died if my father said that to me." Lane's family had readily accepted Maria as part of the family, but there was never any discussion or innuendo about their sex life.

Kyle chuckled. "I never thought he'd say something like that either. You know there's that mutual unspoken denial that your parents or your kids ever have sex. That's not true in my family. Dad said I look great."

Lane relaxed. "I'll second that. You are great. You smell great, and sound great, and feel great. You know, I'd be happy to help you with the getting laid part."

A flush of desire raced through Kyle at the sultry tone of Lane's voice. "Thanks, you were pretty amazing yourself." The image of Lane writhing on her bed flashed in her mind. "I've been thinking about what you said when I left this morning, and since *I am* a great detective, I've come to the conclusion that you want to see me again."

"Really?"

"Yes, really." Kyle's voice was husky.

"Would you put your reputation on it?"

"I'd rather put my body on you."

Oh man, she's good. "I can't argue against irrefutable evidence now can I?"

"You can, but I can make a very compelling case if I have to."

"Is that a threat or an invitation?"

Touché. Kyle glanced at the clock. It was too early for Hollie to be awake, but she heard the first tentative cries coming from her room down the hall. "Neither, I'm just accepting an already issued invitation."

"Wonderful. But it sounds like somebody needs your attention more than I do right now," Lane said. "Go take care of her and call me later, okay?"

"You got it." This woman was amazing.

❖

Kyle spent the rest of the weekend with Hollie, but her mind kept drifting to Lane. She lost count of the number of times she reached for the phone to call her, but Hollie always had other ideas.

Even when she was exhausted, thoughts of Lane kept Kyle from sleeping. When she closed her eyes, she could smell Lane's arousal, taste her soft skin, hear her cries of pleasure. Her fingers tingled remembering her firm muscular body. When she held Lane in her arms, it was as though she'd been born there.

Kyle arrived at The SandPiper soon after opening time on Monday morning and found a table on the patio, content to watch Lane's sleek movements as she prepared for the day. She hadn't yet noticed Kyle's arrival, so Kyle took the opportunity to gaze openly at the woman who occupied her thoughts.

Lane was chatting with a group of men gathered for a breakfast meeting. Long, smooth, muscular legs snaked out of pressed khaki shorts. Kyle swallowed hard as she remembered those legs wrapped around her thigh in passion. The sleeves of Lane's white long sleeve T-shirt were pushed up, revealing strong, tanned forearms. When she leaned down to listen to one of the customers, every pair of eyes at the table dropped to the front of her shirt.

Lane's manner was that of a woman confident in her own skin. Envisioning that skin beneath the loose fitting clothes, Kyle licked her lips and her blood pulse increased it's already rapid tempo. Her eyes were not the only ones following Lane around the patio. But she knew things the other admirers didn't. Like what her skin felt like and tasted like. How it quivered when she approached orgasm, and how she trembled for long minutes after. Behind her dark sunglasses she watched Lane. *I know what you like, what your body craves, and how you respond to my touch in those special places. You're absolutely beautiful. Turn around. Look at me and see that I know these things about you.*

At that moment, Lane turned and stopped in mid-stride. Color rushed to her cheeks.

Kyle smiled at her, and for several long seconds it seemed as if they were completely alone, recognizing that nothing else mattered but each other. The clinking of silverware and the murmur of scattered conversations disappeared. The sound of the waves gently cresting on the beach nearby seemed to grow in intensity and matched the rapid beating of her heart. Lane was hers for the taking, and she was going to grab the moment and hold it tightly.

Lane's heart rate soared and her blood raced through her body and settled in the throbbing spot between her legs. Kyle was sitting and seemed so relaxed, with her legs crossed and a sultry smile on her face. The hands that had touched her intimately were wrapped around a coffee cup. Arms that held her tight when she trembled with aftershocks of orgasm were resting on the thighs that pressed up against her in the heat of their passion. The look on Kyle's face mirrored the thoughts that Lane tried unsuccessfully to control all weekend. Her smile broadened as Lane approached.

Lane suspected her desire was showing but she didn't care.

"Good morning, Detective."

God, I love it when she calls me that. "Yes, it is. But Sunday morning was even better."

Lane's face reflected that she too recalled the day. Lane blushed.

"May I join you?"

Kyle held the chair as Lane sat down. She leaned over and whispered. "You can join me for anything anytime." She couldn't stop thinking about the multiple orgasms they'd shared.

"Thank you, I'll have to take you up on that."

"When?" Kyle asked.

Christ, she's cute in her little butch way. I wonder if she's wearing those tight boxer briefs I like so much under those trousers. Lane's mind turned to mush.

"Excuse me?" she responded feebly.

"When do you want to take me up on it? You know, join me?" Kyle took a sip of her coffee in an effort to calm her senses. "We could have dinner, or there's a great exhibit of Michael Yanostang photographs at the Art Museum." She was about to suggest another activity when she was interrupted.

"Or simply a repeat of Saturday night." *Again and again and again.*

"That's always an option." *Breathe Kyle, breathe.*

"How's Hollie?"

"What?" It was Kyle's turn for her mind to stop functioning.

I've got her rattled again. "Hollie, you know. Little girl about a year old. Dark hair, dark eyes. Poopie diapers. Probably calls you Mama." Lane was enjoying giving her a hard time.

Kyle shook her head and snickered. "Oh yeah, poopie diapers, I remember now. She's fine, thanks for asking."

Lane leaned over and removed the sunglasses that hid the

eyes that could see into her soul. "Take these off. I want to see your eyes."

"Why?" Kyle's voice cracked when Lane's fingers lightly brushed her temples.

"Because they're your most revealing feature."

Kyle scowled, faking concern. "Hmm. That's not good. To be effective I'm supposed to be unreadable."

Lane read something entirely else into her comment. She leaned in closer. "Well, Detective, let me assure you, you are *very* effective." Kyle smiled shyly. "But I wouldn't try interrogating someone you're sleeping with. Your eyes definitely give you away."

"I'll remember that. Now about my original question. When can I see you again?" *All of you.*

There was no sense in beating around the bush. "Your schedule is a little more complicated than mine," Lane said. "You tell me."

"How about dinner tonight? I have the duty for Travis. He's got some school thing to go to, and his wife threatened to kill him if he missed it."

Lane recalled Kyle talking about her partner and how close they were on and off the job. She'd enjoyed her brief conversation with Travis many weeks ago and had a feeling she would like the man. "Dinner sounds great. Do you cook?"

"Yes, but I think I'd be thoroughly intimidated to cook for you," Kyle said. "You do own a restaurant and I've seen your kitchen, remember?"

Lane did remember and suddenly wanted to share it with her. "I wasn't suggesting that *you* cook, I was going to cook and wanted you to help."

"Thank goodness, 'cause I would really have had a bad case of performance anxiety." Kyle stated in mock exaggeration.

"Well, we can't have that now can we? We might have to find something else to do if that happened." Lane stood too quickly for Kyle to follow. She leaned down and placed a quick kiss on her cheek. "Don't get up. Come by around six."

"I'll be there."

Lane bent low and whispered in her ear, "Keep the streets safe, Detective."

CHAPTER ELEVEN

L ane practically jumped on her as soon as she stepped in the front door. Before she had a chance to react, she was locked in a passionate embrace that almost knocked her off her feet. Hands and lips were everywhere and clothes were being pushed aside.

"Does this mean we're not going to eat first?" Kyle asked.

Lane took her by the hand and led her to the bedroom. "Oh, we're definitely not going to eat first." She didn't wait for their clothes to be removed before straddling Kyle on the bed. "I've thought of this all day, and if you don't touch me right now, I'm going to go off without you."

The desire in her eyes told Kyle just how close she was. As Lane claimed her mouth in a hard kiss, Kyle managed to get her hand between their bodies and into the unbuttoned pants. Lane bit her tongue when her fingers unerringly found their mark. Her mind started to spin and her senses focused on the wonderful feeling coursing through her body. Lane wanted it now and she wanted it fast, and the words she whispered in Kyle's ear became reality.

Kyle held her tight as she struggled to catch her breath. She was still trembling when she lifted her head from where it had fallen on Kyle's shoulder when her orgasm overtook her.

Lane tenderly placed kisses on the lips she had ravaged

moments earlier. "Sorry about that. I was okay until I saw you and then I had to have you right then." She chuckled. "Technically, I guess I needed *you* to have *me*."

Kyle caressed the soft cheek above her. "I'm not really a stickler for technicalities. Besides, you did."

It took a moment for Kyle's admission to work its way through Lane's passion drugged brain. When it did she smiled teasingly. "Then I guess we can eat now."

Kyle surprised her when she hopped out of bed and headed toward the kitchen. "Great, I'm starved."

Lane lay where she was, astounded that Kyle had left her so fast. She pulled her clothes together and walked down the hall uncertain if she should be hurt by Kyle's apparently cool treatment. Sure, she had surprised Kyle by jumping on her the minute she stepped inside and used her to assuage her own carnal need, but she didn't expect this.

Kyle was sitting on the couch when Lane entered the room. Her shoes were off and her feet were propped up on the coffee table in front of her next to her service weapon. She looked perfectly relaxed and unflustered by the past fifteen minutes. Lane frowned as she turned toward the kitchen.

"Lane?"

"Yes?"

"Come here for a sec will you?"

Lane didn't know what to expect as she stood in front of her. She kept her eyes focused on the floor and shrieked when Kyle grabbed her hand and pulled her down on the couch and immediately rolled on top of her. She made short work of the clothes that were a barrier to what she sought. Her hands moved confidently over Lane's flushed skin, and her mouth quickly followed, lingering on those areas that fueled Lane's passion. Soon, they were both on the verge of orgasm again, and Kyle slipped off the couch and knelt on the floor. She pulled Lane to her and placed her legs over her shoulders. Staring at her glistening center in the bright light of day, she thought, *Oh Christ, she's beautiful.*

"Kyle, please." Lane was terribly close and she wanted to feel Kyle's tongue on her as she came.

"Paybacks are hell," Kyle said thickly.

For a few aching seconds she withheld relief, but in the end she did not disappoint her. Lane came with an incredible force that almost knocked Kyle over. She screamed Kyle's name and collapsed back on to the couch.

Kyle licked every drop of Lane's passion as she gently quieted her with her tongue. She lifted her gaze and met eyes that were bluer than any she'd ever seen. Lane was up on her elbows, watching her. Their eyes remained locked as Kyle started to move her tongue once again. She slowly licked and sucked and nibbled on the sensitive tissue, pausing only to demand, "Don't close your eyes. Please, I want to watch your eyes when you come."

Lane had never been asked to do such a thing, and she was slightly embarrassed by the idea. *Oh, for Christ's sake. The woman has her mouth on you in the most intimate way. What's to be embarrassed about?* However, as she came closer and closer to the pinnacle moment, it was increasingly difficult to keep her eyes open. She wanted to drift away in the sensations that this wonderful woman was giving her, and with her last bit of effort she focused and climaxed once again.

Kyle was astounded as she watched Lane's face go from pleasure to concentration and back to sheer pleasure again. As long as she lived, she knew she would never see anything more beautiful. She drew Lane into her arms.

Lane snuggled close. "Well that answers that."

"What?" Kyle softly stroked her lover's arms.

"I thought I'd done something wrong earlier."

Kyle pulled back and looked directly into Lane's eyes. "Whatever gave you that idea?" She searched her brain trying to figure out if she had missed a clue or something.

"It's silly, forget I mentioned it." Lane started to get up.

"No, you mentioned it so it must be something that bothered you. I want to know. I need to know."

The pleading in Kyle's eyes gave Lane the courage she needed. "Before, in the bedroom. You just got up like you were more interested in eating than in being with me."

Kyle looked surprised.

"Well, you did!"

"I'm sorry." Kyle laughed and drew Lane close, kissing the tip of her nose. That wasn't my intention at all. I was teasing you. Well I was trying to tease you and I guess it backfired. The way you pounced on me, which by the way made me crazy, fogged my brain. I guess we'd better get to know each other a little bit better before I try that again."

"It made you crazy?" Lane's pulse raced against her skin.

"Oh, yes. It definitely made me crazy. Couldn't you tell?"

Lane blushed. "I was a little caught up in it all," she said by way of apology.

"I'll take that as a compliment. Now, as much as I'd like to ravish you again, I really am starving."

The smile Kyle gave her made Lane's knees go weak again. She took a deep breath and stepped out of the warm embrace. Her naked body immediately missed the warmth of Kyle's flesh. She couldn't get enough of her.

"Then I guess I'd better put some clothes on and feed you."

For the second time in a few short minutes Kyle straightened her clothes. Her panties were soaked from her excitement of being with Lane, and before she could decide whether or not to remove them or tough it out, Lane reappeared wearing thread bare sweat pants and a T-shirt cut just above her belly button. Kyle's passion rose again, this time accompanied with a tenderness that she didn't expect. Lane's choice of clothes, though sexy and revealing, cast a sense of wholesome innocence that ignited in Kyle a fierce sense of wanting to protect her from the ugliness of the world. It was silly she knew. Lane had proven she was perfectly capable of taking care of herself but Kyle wanted to just the same.

Lane couldn't miss Kyle's reaction. She hadn't intended to elicit a rise in Kyle, she had simply grabbed the first thing she found in her dresser drawer. However, she did file it away for future reference.

"Come on, hold that thought and come help me with dinner."

Somewhere between putting the third and fourth layer of pasta in the lasagna pan, Lane rubbed suggestively against Kyle and found herself pinned between the hard, hot body she longed for and the equally hard, but cool counter. She wrapped her arms around Kyle's neck and held on for dear life. Kyle's mouth and hands were everywhere at once, and she was hotter than the temperature of the oven.

"If you want to do this properly, the lasagna takes an hour to cook," Lane said. "We can finish up and move this to the bedroom."

"Are you telling me I'm not doing this properly?" Kyle slid her hand under the waistband of the sweatpants Lane had donned earlier. Her fingers found their mark and slipped easily inside before Lane had a chance to answer.

When she did answer it was barely more than a gasp and a tightening of her arms around Kyle's neck. "No, you're doing it…ugh…perfectly."

JULIE CANNON

Kyle slowly slid her fingers out and circled the tight ridge of flesh that made Lane shudder. "Do you want me to stop so you can finish making dinner?"

She nibbled on Lane's neck as she waited for her reply. Lane tensed and shuddered against her.

"Yes, you can stop. I think you know I'm finished. At least for now."

Knowing how much Kyle desired her made her feel beautiful. The way Kyle touched her was different than the way she had ever been touched before. Yes, the mechanics were generally the same, but the emotions Kyle evoked were very different. The woman was definitely not what Lane had expected.

Kyle reluctantly released her but still stayed close. "Next time I think I'd better eat before I come over for dinner. We'll never get through this at the rate we're going. And if you keep looking at me like that, I'm going to need all the strength I can get." The craving they shared was typical of "new lust" as Kyle often referred to it, but her desire for the woman standing in front of her was very different and she still wasn't sure exactly what it was.

"I could say the same about you, Detective. We'd better be careful. I'd hate for someone to find us naked on the floor, dead from starvation. Why don't you set the table and put some music on while I finish this. Maybe that will keep you out of trouble."

"Keep *me* out of trouble?" Kyle asked incredulously. "I seem to recall *you* were the one who jumped me the instant the door closed, and *you* were the one who rubbed up against me a few minutes ago. What's a poor, defenseless girl to do?" Kyle strolled to the dining room table and held up a fork in each hand.

Lane threw a pasta slice at her, hitting her right in the center of her chest. "You? Defenseless? Detective, you may have used that tactic on other women, but it doesn't fly with this one."

"No? Somehow I really didn't think it would." Kyle plucked the pasta off her shirt determined to find out exactly what would convince Lane she was becoming completely defenseless when it came to her.

❖

"Homicide, Bain." Kyle was distracted.

"Detective Bain, you sound sexy when you answer the phone like that." Lane had taken a chance that Kyle would be available to talk to her.

Kyle smiled at the interruption and set her pencil down on the desk blotter. "No I don't."

Lane laughed. "Oh, yes you do."

Kyle saw Travis looking at her with a knowing grin. "You must be thinking about someone else."

"I've been thinking about you, and what I'd like to do with you."

Lane's voice was husky and Kyle felt her crotch instantly become damp. She turned her chair for some semblance of privacy. "Care to elaborate, Miss Connor?"

She knew Travis was listening even though he pretended not to. But she didn't care. He had already made his assumptions and she'd done nothing to dispel them.

"I don't think you really want me to do that, Detective. You might have difficulty finishing your shift, and I want to see you tonight." Lane knew exactly what she wanted to do with Kyle that evening, and she was certain that she would get no resistance from the woman on the other end of the line.

"Pretty sure of yourself aren't you?"

"Actually, yes I am, and I think you know it." Lane was thoroughly enjoying this banter. It had been a long time since she'd had a lover, and she liked the playful moments she had with Kyle.

"Okay, I give up. I take it from this call that we're doing something this evening." *And if you don't have something in mind, I certainly do.*

"Yes. I'd like you to take me to dinner. I'm in the mood for something spicy, like Thai food. Sound like something you might be interested in?"

"Definitely. I'll let Gretchen know. Seven o'clock?"

"Make it six. I have plans for you after dinner."

Holy shit! "I'll see you at five-thirty."

Kyle heard Lane's quick intake of breath before she laughed. They said good-bye, and she tried to get back to work. Thankfully, Travis pulled her attention away from thoughts about Lane with a question.

"Did you hear from the DA?"

"No, he said he would call today with an update on Williams' plea." Karime Williams had confessed to the murder of his "bitch" Gloria Faulkner. She had been skimming money from him, and when he found out, he became enraged and killed her. He had absolutely no remorse about killing her other than as Gloria's pimp, her death put a large dent in his incoming cash flow. Kyle prayed she would never become as immune to life as this man was. There was a moment during the interrogation when Kyle was tempted to smack his cavalier attitude right off his smug, pockmarked face. Williams had offered up information about a major supplier of cocaine into Los Angeles in return for a reduced sentence. Even with the deal, it was one more killer off the streets.

"You and Lane seeing a lot of each other?"

The change of topic caught Kyle off guard. "You know we are Travis." Kyle looked at her partner knowing he was fishing for more specific information. She was in a good mood and decided to cut him some slack. "She's quite a woman."

"I can tell. You've been walking around here like absolutely nothing in the world could rain on your day. I haven't seen that look on your face in a long time."

"It has been a long time, hasn't it?" Kyle admitted

"Yes it has, and it looks good on you." Travis replied sincerely.

"Thanks. It feels kinda good too." Kyle broke into a grin and threw a paperclip across the desks at her partner.

"Amen to that sister."

❖

Kyle checked her watch as she knocked on Lane's door. She was fifteen minutes early. She was anxious and after four trips around the block she couldn't wait any longer. She studied her reflection in the glass of the front door one more time. She'd thought of nothing but Lane for the past few days and couldn't wait to see her again. She admitted to herself earlier that day that she couldn't wait to get her hands on Lane again as well.

Holy Mother of God! Kyle stood there unable to move at the sight. She knew her mouth was probably hanging open but she didn't care. All she could think about was the beautiful woman standing in front of her wearing nothing but a smile.

"Aren't you going to come in Detective?"

Kyle regained what was left of her equilibrium and stepped across the threshold. Lane didn't move and Kyle's arm brushed her erect nipples as she passed. She didn't get much further when she heard the door shut and the lock click behind her. She turned around and was met with the hot, radiating look of desire that left her in no doubt as to what she could expect. As if Lane opening the door stark naked didn't make it crystal clear.

"We seem to have trouble getting to dinner on time." Her throat was dry and her voice cracked with the effort of forming the words.

"Are you complaining? Because if you are, I can get dressed and we can go now."

Lane took a deep breath which drew Kyle's attention to her breasts. "Hell no. This is a dream come true." Kyle imagined her tongue on the pert nipples.

Lane's nipples hardened into painful tight buds, and she stepped so close to Kyle that her breasts touched the starched pink shirt. "Do you have any other dreams you'd like me to fulfill?"

Kyle's eyes never left the white, soft skin as she slowly lowered her head. "As a matter of fact, I do."

Lane wrapped her arms around Kyle's neck as she was carried into the bedroom. She didn't feel the scratchy bedspread beneath her as she watched Kyle slowly remove her clothes. Kyle's body amazed her; there was real strength hidden beneath the womanly curves, yet her touch was as light as a feather. Lane reached for her before she was fully disrobed. Kyle fell on top of her pinning her body to the bed. The muscles in Kyle's back felt tense beneath Lane's fingers.

"You are so incredibly beautiful." Kyle whispered. She had used this same phrase many times but these were the only words that even came close to conveying her feelings.

Her kisses covered every inch of Lane's body before she returned to the lips eagerly awaiting hers. Lane clutched her tightly and sucked her tongue harder as Kyle nudged her thighs apart. When Lane began to move against her, she took possession of Lane's nipple between her fingers tweaking it in time with the thrusts on her thigh.

Lane wrenched her lips from Kyle's and cried out in a voice

hoarse with desire. "Oh, yes. Don't stop. That makes me crazy."

The path between her nipples and clitoris was a direct connection, and Kyle knew exactly what to do to burn the trail. Lane gasped and arched her back when Kyle's mouth claimed her nipple and her fingers entered. She bit down on her lip in a failed attempt to hold back the impending wave of pleasure. Within a few well timed strokes, she came hard and fast in Kyle's hand, shuddering with the power of her orgasm.

Kyle's hand was trapped between Lane's thighs, and she squeezed it so tightly Kyle started to see stars. Not wanting to ruin the moment but fearing that Lane would damage her gun hand, she lifted her lips from Lane's breast. "Lane, I'm sorry but you're crushing my hand." Lane slowly removed Kyle's fingers from inside her and held Kyle's hand gently as the aftershocks shook her body. Kyle held her close while she slowly regained control. When her ragged breathing slowed to its normal pace, Kyle placed light, feathery kisses along her jaw line.

"Feel better now?"

"Mmm." Lane purred.

"And that translates to?" Kyle asked mockingly.

Lane slapped Kyle on the butt. "You know exactly what that translates to. I don't have to spell it out for you. Or do I?"

Kyle continued her kisses and her hands began to wander again. "No, but I like it when you do."

"Really? I hadn't noticed." Between Kyle's tickling tongue and her insistent hands, Lane was beginning to loose her concentration again. She gasped when Kyle's tongue found her sensitive nipple.

Kyle answered her between nips. "It drives me crazy when you tell me what you want me to do to you." Lane's uninhibited response to her lovemaking was, by far, the most erotic thing she had ever experienced. Sometimes all it took was a single word or sound to send her over the edge.

Each time they made love, Lane learned a little bit more about Kyle. After the first initial explosion, their lovemaking was usually calmer, and it was during those times she noticed Kyle's arousal escalate.

"You mean when I sigh like this?" Lane lightly demonstrated at the same time her hand cupped Kyle's breast. She could almost hear Kyle's desire intensify. "Or when I do this?" Kyle moaned when her fingertips grasped an erect nipple. "Or…" Lane moved her hand much lower. "…When I whisper, 'touch me?'" There was an immediate shift in Kyle when her fingers did exactly what her mouth described. Kyle's juices increased as Lane poised her index finger just at the entrance to the warm, wet center of her desire. "And do you like it when I tell you to go in me?"

Kyle pulled Lane to her and ravaged her mouth with a kiss that served as her answer. She sucked Lane's tongue and matched her rhythm to Lane's fingers as they slowly moved in and out of her. Lane moaned again and Kyle lifted her hips in anticipation of more to come. As her passion climbed, Lane increased the tempo of her fingers to match. Soon, Kyle was moaning her delight as she crested in the arms of her lover.

Lane was humbled that this wonderful woman felt safe enough to be totally exposed while in her arms. Lane suspected that it was difficult for Kyle, whose job it was to maintain absolute control at all times, to let go and be vulnerable. She cradled her gently as the storm subsided.

❖

Between the laughter and sexual innuendo tossed back and forth across the table, Kyle didn't know if she wanted the evening to go on or take Lane home and make love to her all night. She reached for the bill. A movement in the corner of her eye drew her attention away from Lane who sat sipping the remaining wine in her glass. She stood up as a strikingly handsome woman stopped beside their table.

"Stephanie, how are you?" Kyle quickly made the introductions, describing Stephanie to Lane as a "good friend."

In fact, their friendship was a little unusual in that it involved sex, and as soon as Lane looked at Stephanie, Kyle could tell that she'd guessed that somehow. Her smile was lukewarm as the usual pleasantries were exchanged.

"I don't want to intrude, and I have someone waiting for me," Stephanie said. "I just wanted to stop by and say hello. It was good to see you again Kyle."

After she'd walked away, Lane asked, "Are you still sleeping with her?"

Kyle met her eyes squarely, not surprised at the question. "No."

Lane didn't like the feeling of jealousy that had crept into her stomach. "How long were you involved?"

Kyle dropped her eyes. She'd met Stephanie Walker three years ago at an accident scene. Stephanie was a firefighter, and they'd naturally gravitated together due to their stressful jobs and unusual hours. They'd fallen into an easy liaison, each providing comfort whenever the other needed it. Kyle had not seen Stephanie since shortly before Lane returned to The SandPiper. She wasn't ashamed about her relationship with Stephanie or any of the women she'd been with, but she didn't know how to make Lane understand.

"We weren't actually involved."

Lane waited until Kyle lifted her eyes to her again. She tried not to sound accusatory. "Then what were you?"

Kyle toyed with her wine glass. "It's kind of hard to explain."

"Then don't." As much as Lane was curious about the

nature of their relationship, she was not going to force Kyle into disclosing it no matter how much she wanted to know.

"No, I want to. I have to." Kyle struggled to find the right words. "Stephanie is a firefighter and as much as we try to distance ourselves from our jobs, sometimes it gets to us. It's difficult for people to understand what we go through, what we see every day. Sometimes you just need a release from the nightmare. Neither one of us had been seriously involved with anyone, and we...got together from time to time."

Lane frowned and thought about what Kyle said but also what she didn't say. "To release some stress?"

Kyle nodded her head.

"Are you fuck buddies?" Lane continued.

Kyle's head jerked up. "No. No, it's not like that at all. Every day we see the horrible things that human beings can do to each other, and some of those things just don't go away."

Kyle had never tried to explain the emotional effects of her job and she was struggling, but it seemed critical that she make Lane understand.

"We close our eyes and we see mutilated bodies, raped women, and beaten kids. Sometimes we just need to escape, to forget what we've seen and focus on something good and pure. It's like a rebirth. It washes the scum and ugliness out of our lives, or at least it does for that moment." Kyle refilled her glass. "I don't know if you can understand, but it was never sordid or dirty or something that either one of us is ashamed about. Sometimes it wasn't even sex. Sometimes we just needed someone to hold us when we cried. Just two people leaning on each other."

Lane did understand. The simplicity in Kyle's words and honesty in her eyes told her what she needed to know. She wasn't jealous and she wasn't threatened. "I understand."

"I'll always be there for her, Lane."

Lane understood that Kyle's comment was a statement of fact, and she continued to be impressed with this woman's character. "I wouldn't expect anything less from you."

"I'll be there, but I won't sleep with her while we're seeing each other." Kyle had to make sure there was no misunderstanding.

"I have no right to ask that of you." *But as God as my witness I want to.*

Kyle's heart swelled knowing that any other woman would have told her to stop sleeping with Stephanie, but Lane didn't. "I'm seeing *you* now Lane, and I'm not going to sleep with anyone else while I'm with you."

Lane reached over and took Kyle's hand, oblivious to the looks the gesture caused. The candlelight cast a warm glow on her face and brightened the fire in her eyes. "Thank you."

God this woman is wonderful. Kyle drank in the fierce possessiveness in Lane's eyes. She had never felt *owned* before, and it felt surprisingly good, very good. Kyle wanted to see that look every time Lane's eyes met hers. The shadows flickering across Lane's face beckoned Kyle to lightly stroke their pattern, but her hand was held firm in Lane's warm grasp. A shiver ran down her spine as Lane lightly caressed the back of her hand. She watched as Lane ran the fingers of her other hand up and down the stem of her wine glass like a pianist stroking the ivory keys. The slow, seductive strokes transfixed her, and she could almost feel Lane's hands running up and down her back. A lump rose in her throat. Words eluded her.

The soft rise and fall of Lane's chest drew her attention away from the wine glass. Lane had chosen a deep purple blouse with full sleeves and pearl buttons cascading down the front from a mandarin collar. Kyle's hands tingled remembering the soft silkiness of the blouse when she took Lane in her arms and kissed her an hour ago. Those lips, still slightly swollen from their kisses, were wet and inviting, and Kyle ached to cover them again.

Lane's hair was down, a style Kyle had only seen once before, and she was breathtaking. Her understated elegance and sophistication turned heads everywhere they went, and tonight was no exception. She pushed a few errant strands of hair away from her face and Kyle almost stopped breathing. Lane's hands seemed to slide through the air as if they were floating. Everything about her was accentuated and came into sharp focus. Kyle saw more than she'd ever seen before, more than simply her physical loveliness. An inner beauty surrounded her, revealing itself in the play of expressions on her face, the unconscious grace of her body language, and the tenderness of her smile.

Lane's gaze drifted across her like a soft feather brushing her skin. Kyle met her sparkling eyes and for a long while they stared directly at one another.

"I want to make love to you." Kyle said. This time when she said "make love" the words had an entirely different meaning. She saw secrets and promises in Lane, depths she wanted to explore. She wanted to spend a lifetime uncovering all that was still concealed from her.

Lane smiled. "I think we could use a night off. Don't you?" She'd noticed that in addition to being sexy, Kyle sounded tired. Although she wanted to hold her again and spend hours in mutual bliss, there would be time for that later. She wasn't going anywhere, and it was obvious that Kyle wasn't either. Kyle laughed, feeling wonderful realizing that this was what it was all about. Loving someone was more than passion and the unending craving for each other. It was much simpler than that. It was about caring for someone and knowing that what you have is far deeper and sustaining than the physical act of sex. That was just the icing on the cake.

"I hate the idea," she said. "But I see your point."

"I'll expect you to make up for it, of course."

"That'll be torture. How do I volunteer?"

Lane leaned closer and brushed her lips across Kyle's. "My place. Tomorrow evening."

Kyle regarded her warmly. "Do you have any plans for tomorrow, during the day?"

"None that I can't change." Most Saturdays, she followed the same routine; she straightened up around the house and went to the gym.

"Hollie and I are going to the zoo. Would you like to join us?"

Lane hesitated. As she learned more and more about Kyle, she suspected she didn't do anything of importance without thinking it through. The sheer nature of her job demanded it, and her deliberate inclusion of people in Hollie's life verified it. The decision to introduce Lane to her daughter would not have been taken lightly.

Acknowledging the important step, Lane kissed her on the cheek and said, "Thank you. I'd love to. I haven't been to the zoo in years."

CHAPTER TWELVE

K yle was nervous, but thankfully Hollie was too excited about going to the zoo to pick up on her mother's anxiety. It was time to introduce the two most important girls in her life. Kyle didn't want to split her free time between them, but she was adamant that she would not bring someone into Hollie's life unless the relationship was serious. She hoped their first encounter would not be a disaster; she'd heard horror stories. Children could change the dynamic between adults in many different ways and create distractions some women certainly wouldn't want to sign up for. Kyle couldn't imagine Lane being discouraged by a few initial glitches, if they happened. But Hollie was at that stage where she was shy around people and clung to Kyle until she warmed up to a new person. It was quite possible that she would want nothing to do with Lane for a while.

When the doorbell rang, Kyle's trepidations almost outweighed the thrill she felt at the thought of seeing Lane again. Holding Hollie close to her for reassurance, she opened the door and was startled when Hollie almost lunged from her arms at her first glimpse of Lane.

"Whoa, there little one." Kyle tightened her grip.

"It's okay," Lane reached for Hollie and held her as though she'd been doing it for years. "She definitely takes after you, jumping into my arms before I even get in the front door."

"I guess she's as anxious to see you as I am."

Lane leaned over and placed a quick kiss on Kyle's lips. "Are you going to invite me in?"

Laughing, Kyle stepped back from the doorway. "Ignore me. My incredibly shy daughter just decided to be your new best friend. That's okay. I can cope."

She continued to be amazed at how comfortable Hollie was with Lane. They sat down in the living room, and Hollie immediately climbed off Lane's lap and toddled over to pick up a stuffed dog. She hurried back, lifting her arms in the universal symbol for pick-me-up, then snuggled into Lane's lap as if Kyle wasn't in the room. Normally, she seldom let Kyle out of her sight, but she hadn't given her a second glance since Lane arrived.

Stunned, and incredibly relieved, Kyle settled back at her end of the couch and enjoyed watching the two have fun. There was nothing phony in the way Lane interacted with Hollie. She seemed genuinely smitten. *The connection between these two is amazing.*

Things only got better as the day progressed. The excursion turned out to be as perfect as Kyle hoped. Hollie alternated between her and Lane, delighted to be the center of attention. Lane didn't have much experience pushing a stroller, and all three of them laughed as she maneuvered Hollie through the maze of people at the zoo. Lane was showing Hollie the giraffes when Kyle saw another lesbian couple with their two children. They nodded in recognition, obviously assuming Hollie was her and Lane's child.

Kyle felt a sense of pride and camaraderie with the other women. She knew she wasn't the only lesbian raising a child, but she had not imagined she could be like the women who nodded to her—part of a *couple* raising Hollie. Until now, she had thought that putting Hollie first meant she could not have a relationship with a woman, that somehow she would have to choose between the two.

Could she do it? Was she capable of managing the demands of her job, her child, and her lover? She was not naïve. It would be hard, very hard, if it worked at all. Relationships took time, effort, and just pure hard work, and even then most didn't work out. The thought of throwing in the added challenge of shared parenting made Kyle's head spin. And what about the effect of the relationship on Hollie? Would she be ridiculed or ostracized in school because she had two moms? Would other mothers out of fear or ignorance forbid their children from coming to their house to play? Would Hollie some day resent her? Kyle watched Lane lift Hollie high so she could see into a monkey enclosure. Was this the woman she wanted to risk everything for?

The same questions bounced through her mind throughout the long stroll around the zoo and later that day after they returned home. Kyle cherished every moment she had with her daughter and wondered if she would be able to share Hollie with someone. It would be an equal partnership in raising her daughter—their daughter. As she prepared Hollie for her nap, she tried to imagine giving up control and making compromises in areas she may not want to. Could she trust someone else with her sister's child? She had promised Alison she would take care of Hollie. Could she do it? Should she do it? Was Lane worth it?

She kissed Hollie on the forehead and laid the sleeping child in her crib. Everything was changing so quickly, and she felt a little disoriented as she returned to the living room. Lane was sitting on the couch, her head tilted back and her eyes closed.

Kyle touched her lightly on the shoulder. "She's down for the count."

Lane barely moved. Her eyelids fluttered open and she gazed up at Kyle with weary contentment. "I'm beat. I don't remember being this exhausted when I took my nephews to the zoo. Where do they get their energy?"

"I said the same thing when I first brought Hollie home," Kyle said. "I don't know where the energy comes from, but if I could bottle it, I wouldn't be a cop, that's for sure. Can I get you anything?"

"Just your hands." When Kyle's eyes lit up, Lane added, "On my feet. They're killing me." She let her head loll back further. She was tired but invigorated at the same time. She'd been nervous about the day, but Hollie was a wonderful child. Spending time with her was a real pleasure.

Kyle laughed and pulled Lane's feet into her lap. "Whew, I'm glad you clarified that. After chasing the two of you around all morning, I don't think I would have been up to my normal sexual prowess."

She removed Lane's shoes and was rewarded with a moan of pleasure when she started massaging her feet.

Lane wiggled her toes in contentment. "Something tells me, Detective, that you'd be up to your normal mind-blowing, earth-shattering lovemaking standards even if you were absolutely exhausted."

Kyle arched her eyebrows. "Mind-blowing?"

"Among other things." Lane's blood began to race and the familiar tickle began in the pit of her stomach.

Their eyes met. Kyle's were dark with desire. Her hands drifted to Lane's calves and her voice became husky. "Such as?"

Lane shifted her foot so that her heel pressed into Kyle's crotch. The change in Kyle's eyes told her she hit the right spot. "Such as how long does your darling daughter sleep?"

"Long enough."

Kyle gave up the fight to control her own rising tide of desire. Abandoning the massage, she shifted on the couch, pinning

Lane beneath her. She growled as Lane pulled her shirt out of her shorts and ran her nails seductively up and down her back. Kyle quickly made short work of Lane's shirt and bra and dipped her head to capture an erect nipple. Her energy level recharged as she felt Lane respond to her touch. She kissed and caressed every inch of the soft skin and teased the nipple with her tongue. Just as she was about to slide her hand inside the waistband of Lane's shorts, she felt Lane tense. An instant later, Hollie's cries penetrated her passion filled brain. She stopped her movements and drew a ragged breath. Against an erect nipple she murmured. "I guess I forgot to tell her."

Lane surprised her when she started laughing. "Does she always have such good timing?"

"I've never had anyone over before to find out." Kyle placed a quick kiss on the flesh screaming for her attention and sat up. Her eyes devoured the half-naked woman on the couch. "Sorry. I'd better go see what she needs."

After Kyle walked away, Lane lay on the soft leather gathering her wits for a few seconds then found her shirt. Her legs felt weak and her stomach in knots as she slid off the couch and followed the sound of crying down the hall. She peeked around the corner so as not to disturb Kyle if she was trying to get the toddler back to sleep. Kyle was holding Hollie, wiping the tears from her chubby little cheeks.

Lane wasn't sure whether to step into the room or back out, worried that her presence might upset Hollie more. But before she could move the little girl beamed at her. Pointing, she tried to say her name, and Lane's heart melted.

"Well, so much for my plan to be firm but kind." She moved to Kyle's side. "She already knows I'm a pushover."

"Lucky me." With a teasing sideways glance, Kyle settled Hollie back in her crib and slowly stroked her head until her eyes dropped closed.

They crept from the room and Lane asked, "How much longer will she sleep."

"Not long enough," Kyle said. "I'll get her up soon. My parents are coming over for dinner."

"I should get going then." Lane hoped her disappointment wasn't obvious.

"No," Kyle said sharply. "I mean will you stay? I'd like you to meet them. I should have asked sooner, but I was…distracted."

Lane stared down at her semi-clad state. "I'm not exactly dressed to meet the parents."

"You look gorgeous. Especially with that unfulfilled sexual desire you have plastered all over your face."

"Oh, thanks. That's really going to impress your family. Anyway, I do not look like that."

"Yes you do look like that. I should know, I feel the same way."

"Hold that thought," Lane said. "I have plans for you later."

"Do you think you can keep your hands to yourself while my parents are here?"

Lane was saved from her next teasing comment by the door bell.

❖

Lane enjoyed the evening immensely. It was obvious that Constance and Michael Bain were close to their daughter and actively involved in their granddaughter's life. The family resemblance between Kyle, her mother, and Hollie was remarkable. The unconditional love and support Kyle received from her parents was clear from the pride on their faces as they asked about her current investigations. Lane found them easy to talk to, and they seemed genuinely interested in The SandPiper. She had the impression that they knew she and Kyle were not just casually dating but that the relationship was serious.

Constance took Hollie away to give her a bath after dinner, and Lane declined Michael's offer to help clean up. Helping Kyle load the dishes into the dishwasher, she said, "I should go."

"Why? Do you have to?"

Lane shook her head. "No, but I'd feel kind of awkward being here when your parents leave." For some strange reason she felt like a teenager caught by her girlfriend's parents having sex.

Kyle stepped closer and took her hands. "Have they said or done something to make you feel uncomfortable?"

"No, not at all. They're wonderful." This was her problem, not something brought on by Kyle's parents.

Kyle scoured Lane's face detecting no trace of anything but the truth. "Lane, I'm a grown woman. They've known that for a long time. They let me live my life and they always have. They wouldn't think it out of the ordinary if they left before you. I can guarantee that they won't think twice about it."

The sincerity in Kyle's voice was unmistakable. Lane's heart swelled with the knowledge that Kyle didn't just humor her, she took her feelings seriously. She realized she was just being silly and pulled Kyle to her for a long, lingering kiss. "You're right about one thing."

Kyle laughed recognizing the familiar teasing in Lane's voice. "Only one?"

Lane ran her thumb over lips swollen from her kiss. "You are most definitely a grown woman. A woman who needs to finish what she started earlier this afternoon. When are they leaving?"

"Not soon enough."

"Not soon enough for what dear?" Constance held her hand

up. "Don't answer that. I know exactly what you would say and I'll say it for you. Your father and I are leaving now, and Hollie told us she wants to spend the night with us."

With her blood racing in the direction of her clit, Kyle was a little slow on the uptake. "She did?"

"Yes, she did. I understood her perfectly. Michael is getting her diaper bag ready, and we'll bring her back tomorrow afternoon after her nap. Is that okay?" Constance looked directly at Lane as she asked the question.

"Sure, Mom, that'd be great."

"That settles it then." When Constance settled something, there was no further discussion. "Now you two come and kiss our little girl good-bye, and we'll get out of your hair."

When the door closed behind them, Kyle broke into peels of laughter as Lane collapsed into the chair.

"I don't think it's funny," Lane said weakly. "I almost died of embarrassment."

When she recovered enough to breathe, Kyle came over and knelt in front of her. "Come on. If you think about it, it's kind of like getting caught under the bleachers in high school. But this time we didn't get in trouble."

Lane suddenly found the humor that had deserted her when Kyle's mother walked in on them. She smiled seductively and opened her legs, inviting Kyle to come closer. "I never got caught under the bleachers."

Kyle's eyes flamed with desire. "Were you ever a cheerleader?"

Smiling seductively, Lane leaned back in the chair and forgot all about babies, mothers, and getting caught.

❖

"Have you thought about what you're going to tell Hollie about her mother when she gets older?"

The question came out of the blue and Kyle thought for a minute about her answer. They were lying in the center of Kyle's bed, a light sheet covering them. After hours of lovemaking, her breathing was finally returning to normal but serious conversation was the last thing on her mind.

"I'll tell her the truth," Kyle replied.

"Did you ever think about having a child of your own… before Hollie?" Lane asked tentatively.

"To tell you the truth, I never really gave it much thought, and now I'm so busy I don't have time to think about it." Kyle gathered strands of Lane's damp hair from her face. "And you?" She held her breath waiting for Lane's answer.

"I don't have the need to bear a child, but I had thought of adopting." Sadness overwhelmed Lane. She had been far too busy concentrating on getting well to think about anything else. With her condition, she'd heard the door slam on her dream of a family. No one would let a woman with her medical history adopt a child, and common sense told her there was good reason for that.

"Really?" Kyle used a subtle interrogation technique to have Lane continue. They hadn't talked this way before, and she sensed that she was touching on difficult emotional territory. Lane burrowed closer into the strong arms that held her as if they could ward off her sadness. "There are thousands of children that need a loving home, and I wanted to provide that for a child, maybe even two or three. I always wanted to be a mom. I thought I could be a pretty good one."

Kyle picked up on Lane's use of the past tense. "You don't want that anymore?" Lane was such a natural with Hollie, Kyle couldn't believe that for a minute. She was already picturing days like today happening permanently.

"No, I want it very much. I just don't see it in my future, long term." Lane tensed, hoping she didn't say too much.

Not quite the answer she was looking for. Kyle asked, "Why not?"

Lane hesitated. This was the perfect time to tell Kyle the entire story about Maria and her heart. She knew that by not telling her she was deceiving Kyle, and she was uncomfortable with that. She took a deep breath but the words wouldn't come out of her mouth. What she was waiting for she didn't know. Or perhaps, if she were honest, she knew exactly why she was holding back. She didn't want this magic to end, and she was afraid if Kyle knew, it would change everything.

She hadn't intended the conversation to go this direction when she asked the original question. She was perfectly content lying in Kyle's arms, and her mind had drifted to their wonderful day. Hollie was a bright, curious, well-mannered child, and more than once Lane found herself thinking of what it would be like if she were the child's mother. She and Maria had talked about having a child, but now Lane couldn't even imagine raising a child with anyone other than Kyle. She tensed at the thought. *Where did that come from?*

Awkwardly, she said, "It's taken all my energy getting back into running the restaurant, and I've had to put myself on hold, in a way. Do you know what I mean?"

"Yes. I did the same thing myself when…we lost Alison. So much happened so fast, I just did what I had to do, and that's how it's been. It's like I put myself away somewhere. I have my roles. Mother. Detective. Family member."

Kyle stopped talking, surprised by the feelings that rushed over her. She hadn't realized how empty she felt in some ways. Blatantly absent were the words lover and partner. Lane's words had made her aware of a core of loneliness she simply took for granted, a sense that she was controlling her life instead of living it.

"Have you thought about what you do want to do?" Kyle asked. "I mean, long term? Are you going to keep the restaurant? Do you want to do anything else?"

Up to this point their conversations had been on the here and now, both of them seeming to avoid any discussion about the future, their future. Kyle was no longer satisfied with that. She wanted them to stop talking like two individuals with totally separate lives and acknowledge that they shared too much to carry on that pretense. The thought shocked her but also thrilled her. She had never imagined feeling this way about someone, having this powerful certainty that their relationship was going somewhere. As Lane's words rolled over her, she made an effort to listen instead of losing herself in crazy imaginings about the future.

"I love The SandPiper. It's my baby and I want to make her as successful as I can. But I'm not quite sure what that means, or if I'll recognize it if I see it. Other than that, I really don't know anymore." Lane's illness had taught her that life was fleeting and every day could be her last. She didn't want to waste another day, but she also didn't know what she wanted to do.

Kyle suspected that most people who recovered from a serious illness looked at life differently. Lane had practically told her as much. "What *did* you want to do? Before you got sick."

Lane felt Kyle's question rumble through her chest. "Live happily ever after."

"Like with two kids and a white picket fence?" Kyle knew the question was not as light-hearted as she'd intended, but she felt Lane smile against her chest.

"And someone who loves me." The words were out before

Lane knew they were coming. She was afraid to move. Afraid to think about what Kyle would say to that. She wanted to run but wanted to stay even more.

"Do you think you can't have that now?"

"I'm not sure," Lane answered honestly.

"I think you can," Kyle said firmly and pulled the blanket over them both.

CHAPTER THIRTEEN

The afternoon at Travis' place was perfect. Even though his two little boys were older than Hollie, they doted on her like she was their little sister. Kyle felt good as she watched her lover and her best friends get to know each other. Joann and Travis filled the conversation with stories of Kyle's various escapades as Travis' partner. Finally, after several hours of half-truths, Kyle decided they'd had enough fun at her expense and she needed to get Lane away from their influence.

The drive back to her house started peacefully. Hollie quickly fell asleep in the back seat, and Kyle held Lane's hand, lost in her own thoughts. She hit the brakes by instinct, barely absorbing that an accident had happened in front of them. She was out the door almost before the car came to a halt.

Tossing her cell phone to Lane, she instructed, "Call 911. Tell them we need an ambulance. Several of them. Now."

Lane watched her lover run to the accident scene unfolding in front of her. She'd been gazing out her side window and had no idea what was happening when she was thrown forward. Her heart pounded as she answered the emergency dispatcher's questions. Three cars had collided. Yes, there were injuries. Horrified, she saw Kyle withdrawing from a mangled blue car, her arms and shirt front covered in blood.

Oh my God. She started to get out of the car to help, but

stopped when she remembered that Hollie was in her car seat. Torn as to whether or not to help Kyle, she was relieved when she heard sirens coming their way.

While the paramedics and fire department worked feverishly to free the trapped occupants, Lane couldn't take her eyes off the woman who had captured her heart. Her strong sense of control wasn't threatened by her need to be held and vulnerable in the arms of her lover. The emergency crews as well as the other police officers deferred to her authority, and she moved briskly and efficiently around the scene. She spoke to each of the victims of the crash as they were pulled from their vehicles and stood quietly over those that had been covered with a sheet.

Sometime during the melee Hollie woke and was looking for her mommy. Lane unbuckled the car seat and lifted her onto her lap. She didn't want Hollie to be frightened if she saw Kyle covered in blood so she kept her distracted. When Kyle finally did approach her car, she had changed into a scrub shirt and her arms were clean.

Kyle leaned down and looked inside the car. "Hey there kumquat. Did you have a good nap?"

Hollie squealed and reached for Kyle, and Lane lifted her through the open window.

She followed the little girl outside. "Are you all right?"

Kyle leaned past Hollie and placed a soft kiss on Lane's lips. "I'm fine, but I'm going to have to be here at least another hour or two while they investigate this mess. Can you take Hollie home for me? She shouldn't be any trouble. I'll let Gretchen know and she can come watch her."

"I'll be happy to take her home." Lane touched Kyle's arm. "There's no need to bother Gretchen. I'll just stay and wait for you."

"You don't have to do that."

"Don't you want me to?" Lane started to feel a chill.

"I don't want you to feel obligated to take care of my child." Kyle sounded harsher than she intended.

The chill instantly turned to heat. "Is that what you think— that I feel *obligated* to take care of your child? Why? Because you're fucking me."

Lane was hurt and she knew she shouldn't be lashing out at Kyle. Not now, not like this and certainly not in front of Hollie. She took a calming breath and rubbed her hands across her face.

Kyle didn't know if she was more stunned by the anger in Lane's voice or her words. *Does she really think that?* Before she had a chance to say anything, Lane spoke again.

"I'm sorry, I shouldn't have said that." She looked at Hollie who was blissfully playing with Kyle's necklace. "Kyle, I don't feel obligated, I want to help. I'm glad you asked me to help and that you trust me enough with your child. At least I think you do."

Kyle put her free arm around Lane. "Of course I trust you. Will you please take Hollie home, and I'd love it if you'd stay with her. I'll get a ride with one of the patrol officers."

"Of course I will." Lane felt more on an even keel now. "Come on, big girl. Let's go home and we can play with Big Bird while we wait for mommy. Okay?"

The little girl smiled and reached for Lane. They both got big kisses from Kyle before they drove off.

❖

It was late when Kyle finally turned the key in her front door. She was tired and dirty and exhausted, and as the prime witness, she'd had to repeat her story to the accident investigators several times. She knew Lane would be waiting for her and, for the first time in a long while, when she stepped across the threshold she felt like she was coming home.

Lane heard the door open and jumped off the couch. She'd given up reading several hours earlier and had been lost in her thoughts. Ever since their conversation about the future, she'd been thinking about how she was going to tell Kyle everything. It was time.

"Hi, welcome home." She wrapped her arms around Kyle's shoulders and gave her a hug. The fatigue in Kyle's bones was evident. "Come on, let's get you showered and into bed."

Kyle stopped her as they walked into the master bath. "I'm sorry about earlier. I was a jerk. I'm not used to having someone like you." She had barely thought of anything else but the ugly words they had exchanged at the accident site.

"Someone like me?" Lane didn't want another argument or misunderstanding.

Kyle stood directly in front of her and took both of her hands. "Someone in my life. I'm very independent, and other than my parents and Travis, there isn't anyone I depend on. And I know that I can rely on you. I like that feeling."

"Me too." That was all Lane had to say about it. "Get clean and come to bed."

Kyle didn't waste any time. She showered and then crawled into bed. As soon as her head hit the pillow of Lane's arm, she knew she could not keep her eyes open. There were things she wanted to say, but even as she began to form the words she felt herself falling asleep.

As she felt Kyle's weight relax against her, Lane dropped a kiss on her hair. She tried to sleep, but her mind whirled with the events of the last few weeks. She'd been unable to relax during the hours before Kyle came home, and even now she still felt slightly jittery. The car wreck had upset her, but that wasn't the only thing. Lane was unsettled. She had the odd sense that if she didn't hold fast to what she had with Kyle, it would slip from her fingers.

Kyle was unlike anyone she had ever known. She was strong and sensitive, warm and witty. She had a quick mind and an exceptional sense of humor. But most importantly, she was honest, had impeccable character, and she loved her daughter. Lane liked the way Kyle treated her. She was respectful and considerate. She held open doors, held her chair when she sat down, and made sure she got to her door safely. On their first date, Lane had alluded to the fact that she was chivalrous, and Detective Kyle Bain was definitely that.

As she lay there quietly, Lane tried to picture her life without Kyle and saw only darkness. The fact that Kyle had a child didn't trouble her. Hollie was wonderful, exactly the kind of daughter Lane had envisioned when she and Maria were starting to talk about adopting, before she got sick. Lane released a long, slow breath. She felt incredibly relieved that she hadn't had a child with Maria. There was absolutely no comparison between her ex and the woman lying asleep in her arms.

Pushing all thoughts of Maria out of her mind, Lane snuggled down into the covers and tightened her hold on Kyle. She kissed the top of her head as she whispered, "I love you."

❖

"Breathe! Breathe! Come on little guy. Please breathe!"

Lane woke, startled by her lover sobbing and screaming for someone to breathe. She laid her hand on Kyle's shoulder and gently shook her. "Kyle, wake up. You're having a dream."

In the half-light from the hall, Kyle's eyes were glazed and filled with fear. She covered them as she sat up. Her skin was clammy and covered with sweat. Lane touched her shoulder tentatively, careful not to startle her. She was frightened of what could upset this woman this much.

"I'm okay." *And embarrassed and ashamed.* Her voice was dry and cracked. "It was just a nightmare. I'm all right now. I need to get some water."

Before Lane could say anything, Kyle was out of bed. She vanished down the hall and was gone for so long that Lane began to worry and pushed the covers off her legs. She was about to get up when Kyle walked in fully composed.

Kyle held a glass of water out. "Would you like some?"

"No, thanks." Lane wasn't certain about what she should do. She didn't know if Kyle wanted her there or not.

Kyle seemed to read her mind. "Please don't go."

Her voice was pained. Those three words were the hardest she'd said in her life. In the time it had taken to get her drink and return to the bedroom, she'd made a decision. She didn't want to be alone. She didn't want to face the nightmare alone anymore. She wanted to feel the comfort of Lane's arms around her as she battled the demons of the fire.

"I'm not going anywhere," Lane said.

She was relieved when Kyle slid into bed and turned into her. With her head in the crook of Lane's shoulder, she started to talk.

"I was driving home one night and there was a house on fire, a group home. It's not politically correct to call them orphanages. We managed to save five kids, but I couldn't save one little boy. One precious little boy named Jacob. There wasn't a scratch on him. He just looked like he was sleeping. But he wasn't. He was dead from smoke inhalation."

Oh Kyle. The pain you must have suffered.

"They gave me a medal and little Jacob got a headstone. I

started having nightmares about a month later." Her voice cracked and Kyle felt tears slide down her cheeks onto Lane's warm flesh. "Two kids died in that car accident tonight."

When Kyle's tears subsided, Lane pulled her into her arms and kissed away the pain and gently made love to her. Lane's caresses were tender yet demanding, making her forget everything except how she felt as she surrendered control. She felt like she was floating on air with all of her senses on high alert. Soon, her body raged with desire and her insides were molten lava. She craved Lane's mouth on her and when she couldn't stand it any longer she told her so.

Lane savored every touch, taste and smell of the woman she loved. She wanted to erase all the pain Kyle ever had and save her from experiencing any more. The love she felt for Kyle exploded within her and she trembled with the knowledge. She gently pressed her mouth to the warm, wet outer lips that awaited her. She nudged her tongue past the folds, and when Kyle called her name, it sent her over the edge. She shuddered with the effect of her own orgasm but concentrated on pleasing Kyle.

She didn't need Kyle to tell her what to do or how to do it. She knew her lover almost better than she knew herself and used that knowledge to its fullest. Flicking her tongue over the soft warm skin that arched toward her, she felt Kyle tense and knew she was an instant away from orgasm. Kyle's hard clitoris peaked against her mouth. Her hips lifted. Her hand clamped down on Lane's head, urging her on. She increased the pressure of her tongue and was rewarded with a scream of fulfillment as Kyle came in her mouth.

❖

Much later, Lane woke alone. She followed the voice that

was coming down the hall. What she saw made her breath catch in her throat. Kyle was in the rocking chair, gently cradling a sleeping Hollie in her arms. She was singing softly to the child so as not to wake her. Lane watched her for several moments before slipping unnoticed back to bed. Anyone else looking at the poignant scene would assume that the mother was comforting the child. But Lane knew it was just the opposite.

CHAPTER FOURTEEN

Hello, Lane."

She froze. The rumble of that familiar voice once made her heart melt and her blood race, but now it just made her cold. She slowly turned around, her face as composed as she felt. "Maria."

"How are you? You look great."

"My health is no longer your concern, Maria."

She was satisfied when her former lover cringed at her bitter words. Outwardly Maria looked exactly the same as she did the last time Lane saw her over a year ago. Her hair was a little longer and held traces of gray, but other than that the only difference was Lane's reaction to seeing her. She felt nothing. Not anger, not spite or even pity for a woman who could be so callous as to abandon her seriously ill lover.

"I've been thinking about you," Maria said.

"Really?" Lane was so distracted by the unexpected appearance of the woman she once loved that she didn't respond when she heard a soft knock on her office door. She was vaguely aware of footsteps in the hall. Whoever it was could wait.

Maria stepped closer. "I've missed you, Lane."

Lane had nothing to say and was not about to encourage any conversation between them. With cool disinterest, she asked, "What are you doing here?"

"I was wondering if we could have dinner." Maria fixed her with the look that used to break her will.

"Why?"

"I've missed you."

Lane shrugged. "You already said that."

Maria swallowed. Her breathing seemed uneven. "I'd like another chance. I'd like to come home."

It took several moments for the words to penetrate. Hundreds of images of their relationship flashed through Lane's mind. "You what?"

Maria reached for her hands. Lane stepped back before she made contact.

"I know I made a mistake. I'm sorry."

At that point Lane lost all semblance of control. "A mistake? Is that all you have to say?"

"I was under a lot of pressure. You got sick and I…I didn't handle it very well." Maria was pleading her case, trying to say the right things so Lane would take her back.

Lane walked to the other side of the small room, determined to regain control of her emotions. It was okay to show her anger, but she didn't want Maria to see how badly she'd been hurt. "*You* didn't handle it very well. Jesus Christ, Maria, *I* was the one who was dying."

"Lane, I said I'm sorry. I made a mistake." The conversation was obviously not going the way Maria had expected.

Lane had often speculated about what her ex would say if she ever returned and it was certainly not this. "Are you nuts? You didn't *make a mistake*. You left me. I was lying in a hospital bed and you fucking left me because *you couldn't handle it*." Her voice gained in volume as she spoke. "You left me there to die. Alone!"

Maria recoiled from the angry words. "Lane, you weren't alone, your family was there."

"You chicken shit," Lane was disgusted that she was once deeply in love with the pathetic woman standing in front of her. Holding back the tears of pain and anger that threatened to overtake her, she said, "You were my family. I loved you. I was going to spend the rest of my life with you. What was I thinking?"

"Lane, please listen. I—"

"Shut up, Maria." Lane took a menacing step forward. "If you think I'd have anything to do with you after what you did to me you are even more stupid and self-centered than I thought."

"Lane, we had eight great years. We were making a life together. We were going to have a child. Don't you have any feelings left for me at all?" Maria's voice was filled with tears.

Lane couldn't believe that she still didn't get it. "Are you out of your fucking mind? Let me spell it out for you. I was dying and you left me. No note, not a word, nothing! I came home from the hospital, to *our* home and you were gone. Along with all the furniture and any sign you'd ever lived there. The only thing you left were dust bunnies and a pile of bills. Now here's the part where it gets tricky, so pay attention. I want *nothing* to do with you and I have *nothing* to say to you. Now get the fuck out of my office before I kick your pathetic, sorry, selfish ass all the way to Mexico."

Maria didn't move.

"Now!" Lane yelled.

This time Maria turned and stepped directly in the path of Detective Kyle Bain.

Lane didn't know how long she'd been standing there, but it was obvious that she'd heard plenty. She looked into the eyes of the woman she left trembling and naked in her bed just a few short hours ago, and said, "Hi. Maria was just leaving."

She wanted to take pleasure in the way comprehension changed Maria's pleading expression to a scowl directed at Kyle.

But she just wanted the woman gone. Out of her restaurant and out of her life. Forever.

Kyle had heard the entire conversation between Lane and her ex, and her heart ached for the pain she must have endured at the hands of that woman. Fixing Maria with a warning stare, she asked, "Can you find your way out or do I need to escort you?"

Without a word, Maria stalked away. As soon as Kyle shut the door behind her, Lane's legs started shaking and she thought she might faint.

"Are you okay?" Kyle waited for Lane to give some indication of what she needed from her.

"I think so." Lane tried to summon up a smile. Suddenly very tired, she sank down onto the couch. "How much did you hear?"

"How much do you want to tell me?" It was up to Lane to decide how much she was willing to disclose, how much pain she wanted to reveal.

"Will you take me home?"

Kyle didn't hesitate. "Yes."

"Will you make love to me?"

"Right now?" Kyle glanced around the office for an appropriate spot if the answer was yes. The desk looked much too hard and the couch was actually a love seat.

Lane finally smiled. "Well, that would be nice, but I was thinking along more traditional lines. My bed, for example. I need to feel you against me."

❖

Ninety minutes later Kyle held a quivering Lane in her arms. Lane's breathing had returned to normal and Kyle pulled the sheet over them.

"Why is it you've never asked me about Maria or any of the women I've been with?"

The question caught Kyle off guard. She thought for a moment before answering. "I don't care about the other women you've slept with. They're in the past and I don't need to know the details unless you want to tell me." It made her crazy to think about someone else touching Lane, so she preferred not to.

"Maria and I had been together for about eight years when I got sick. At first she was a wonderful, caring partner, shuttling me back and forth to the doctor, getting me chicken soup, that sort of thing. But when things got worse and I went into the hospital, her visits got farther and farther apart. In the end I was too sick to know that she wasn't there. My parents and my brother John were with me while she was packing everything she owned and quite a few things she didn't."

"I'm sorry, Lane." The words sounded empty but it was all Kyle knew to say. "When did you find out?"

"About four days after my surgery. John told me. He came here to drag her back to the hospital and found an empty house. Poor guy, he was scared to death to tell me. He had to clear it with my cardiologist first."

Telling Kyle about Maria was a relief, but she was worried about where their relationship would go from here.

Kyle reached down and ran her finger gently down the pink scar on her chest. "Tell me about this." Her tone was gentle and unthreatening.

"I had a heart transplant." The answer was so matter of fact, Lane wasn't sure if she'd even said it.

Kyle tried to control her reaction but failed miserably. "You had what?"

It was too late to decide she didn't want Kyle to know, so Lane told her everything. "I caught a virus that attacked the lining of my heart. At first I thought it was just a cold or the flu, but I never got better. My doctor ran some tests that didn't pinpoint what was wrong, and when I collapsed, I was finally sick enough for the virus to be detected. It was aggressive and by the time they knew what it was, my heart had suffered too much damage. I needed a transplant."

"Jesus, Lane, that's a little more than 'tinkering' as you phrased it." Images of Lane lying in a hospital bed and then lying in a casket jumped into her head. Fear gripped her heart when she realized just how close Lane had come to dying.

"I didn't…I don't want to be treated differently. I'm not sick. My doctor says I'm healthy, and I don't want people gawking at me or treating me as if I'll break."

"Lane, you should have told me."

"Why?"

"Why? What kind of ridiculous question is that? Holy Christ, Lane, you had a heart transplant. It's not like you had your appendix removed."

Lane pushed herself out of Kyle's embrace. She was angry. "And this is the exact reaction I don't want from people. Especially from you." Lane regained control and continued softly. "I don't want this to change the way we are. I don't want you to treat me differently, in bed or out of bed."

She was hopeful and fearful of what she saw in Kyle's eyes. She didn't want their relationship to change, but she knew that it already had.

❖

Kyle sat against the front of the couch with Lane between her legs leaning back against her chest. They were nibbling on grapes and cheese that Lane scrounged from the kitchen. Kyle moved her fingers softly over Lane's skin, gently tracing the reminder that this wonderful woman almost died.

"Do you ever wonder about the donor?" Kyle was still a bit shaken with the news Lane had shared with her earlier. Lane's anger had subsided, and Kyle felt calm enough to ask more questions.

"In the beginning I practically obsessed over it. Who she was, what was she like, did she have a family? Now I just give thanks every day. I think about the loss her family must have felt, and I wonder how they're feeling now. I try to live every day honoring the gift they gave me. I hope they have some peace."

"It was a woman? Do you know anything about her?" Kyle's hands started to drift south.

Lane's fingers stroked the strong legs stretched out on either side of her. "Not much, they keep things pretty confidential. I do know that she was young and died from a brain aneurysm. I think it was somewhere back east because John said it took four or five hours for the heart to get here."

Kyle's head began to spin and the roar in her ears became deafening. Every muscle in her body froze. *No, it can't be.*

Lane felt Kyle's body turn to stone. "Kyle, what is it?

Kyle could barely speak. "When did you have your surgery?"

Lane shifted position, turning to face her. "It was a year in March. Why? Kyle, what is it?"

Kyle gripped her arms so tightly it hurt. The look in her eyes frightened Lane. She hardly recognized the voice that spoke.

"When *exactly*? Tell me!" *Please God. No!*

"March 24th."

Kyle lost all feeling as her world spun out of control. *No, no, no!* She got up and searched frantically for her clothes. "I've got to go." *I've got to get out of here!*

Lane stood up and reached for her. "Kyle, honey what is it? What's going on?"

Kyle jerked away from Lane's touch. "I can't be here. This can't be happening." Her last statement was not directed to Lane but more to herself. Her hands shook so badly she couldn't get her shirt buttons through their respective holes.

"Kyle, for God's sake. Tell me what in the hell is going on!" There was no way Lane was going to let her leave without knowing what happened.

Kyle turned, her face ashen and streaked with tears. The look on her face was one Lane knew she would never forget.

"Alison lived in Connecticut and died of a brain aneurysm after giving birth to Hollie. I signed the authorization to donate her organs, including her heart on March 24th. You got her heart, Lane. You have my twin sister's heart."

❖

Kyle's last words hung in the air: *You have my twin sister's heart.*

Lane was stunned. She replayed the scene in her mind over and over again trying to find the piece that was missing. It didn't make sense. One minute they were sharing an intimate conversation as only lovers can, and the next, Kyle was in a panic and couldn't get away from her fast enough.

As if on automatic pilot, Lane bent down and retrieved the clothes scattered around the room. She'd always been comfortable with nudity and often didn't get dressed all day if she wasn't going to the restaurant or running errands, but she suddenly felt oddly vulnerable. She stepped into her panties and shorts and reached for the bra that had somehow ended up on the other side of the room along with her tank top.

The scene replayed itself in her mind. She had barely closed the door behind Kyle when she was swept into a passionate kiss that made her forget everything except the way she felt in Kyle's embrace. In a matter of seconds her clothes were off, and Kyle's demanding hands and lips were seeking satisfaction.

Lane buckled the front clasp of her rose colored bra. All the pieces started falling together one clink at a time. Her hands froze against the thin vertical seam over the heart that had once beat in another woman's chest.

"No, it can't be," she told the empty room.

The specific details of her donor were confidential, but the key elements were too close to be a coincidence. Or were they? Kyle's sister, Alison, had a brain aneurysm in childbirth. Lane's donor had an aneurysm. Alison had lived in Connecticut. Lane's donor was a woman who lived in the eastern part of the country. She received her new heart on March 24th, the same day Alison's organs were harvested.

Lane's legs refused to support her any longer, and she fell into the overstuffed chair next to the couch where she and Kyle had made love for a second time not thirty minutes earlier. Fear clenched her gut like a vice and she fought a wave of nausea. She ran her shaking hands through her hair, her mind racing in direct competition with her heart.

"This can't be happening. Not now." Not now after all she's been through. She'd come too far.

Lane stumbled off the chair and went outdoors, finally settling in one of the Adirondack chairs on the patio. The warm breeze on her face kept her hair out of her eyes, and she studied the churning ocean. She loved this view. The rise and fall of the waves were so much like the past eighteen months of her life. She'd been happy. She had good friends, a successful business, and what she'd thought back then was a good relationship. That wave crested and crashed when she got sick and Maria left. The next waves consisted of the successes and setbacks in her long road back to complete recovery. But this afternoon, the wave she'd been riding for the past few wonderful weeks crested and came crashing down.

Lane rested her legs on the small patio table and reflected on the past few months. She was happy again and getting stronger every day. She had complete faith in her new heart, and most days never thought it was not the original model. It certainly was not that way in the beginning. For weeks she'd listened for every beat, waiting for the time when the strong thumping would suddenly stop. But it never did, and eventually she accepted it as she would if it were one of the crowns that her dentist had placed over a bad tooth. There were things that she had to do to keep herself alive, and those minor inconveniences were certainly worth it. She controlled her life now and refused to let it control her.

But at what cost? She didn't think she wanted to get seriously involved with someone again. How could she subject a woman to a life of uncertainty? And what if she left when things got difficult? Lane wasn't afraid of being alone, she just didn't want to die alone.

"God damn you, Kyle. I'm the one who's had to go through all this shit." She shouted to the blue sky scrambling out of the chair. "My whole life was changed forever. I'm the one that almost died. I'm the one that has to take pills every fucking day for the rest of my life just to stay alive. I'm the one that this happened to, not you! But you're the one that left. You're no better than Maria. Things get a little tough and you run." Lane stopped pacing and fell back into the chair. "Damn you, Kyle. I thought you were stronger than that. I thought I could depend on you no matter what. I thought we had the beginning of something special. I thought we could work out anything. I thought…" Lane stopped, her voice cracking. "I guess it doesn't matter what I thought. Because this is what I got."

Lane tipped her head back and closed her eyes. Guilt overwhelmed her like a smothering darkness. She was alive. Alison was dead. A child would never know her mother. A wonderful woman lost a sister. Parents lost a daughter. It wasn't all about her. Not at all.

She had fallen in love with Kyle without even being aware it was happening. She fell into her life at a time she wasn't expecting it, and now that she was there, Lane didn't want her to leave. She loved her strength, her warmth, her integrity, and the way she respected her. No one ever looked at her the way Kyle did, and her smile touched Lane deep inside. She was a fabulous, attentive lover, and Lane loved watching the ecstasy spread across her face when they made love. She knew Kyle loved her daughter, her family, her work and Lane suspected she loved her as well.

But cresting waves always crashed. The one thing that gave her life, gave her a second chance at life, might be the one thing that was crushing her now. She couldn't breathe, couldn't think and could almost feel her heart breaking. She wasn't sure she could survive this kind of loss. Was having a new heart worth the pain of a broken heart?

Night fell and the cool air drifted over Lane, driving her inside. She stopped just inside the door. There it was, her answer as big as life, stunning her with its simplicity. A small bouquet of flowers that Kyle had given her this afternoon. It wasn't fancy, nor did it contain exotic flowers from the other side of the world. It was simply an unadorned vase overflowing with white daisies, her favorite. Two long strides took her to the vase, and she lifted it with both hands, deeply inhaling the sweet scent.

It was then and there she knew without a doubt that she loved

Kyle, not the superficial love she had with Maria, but the deep, abiding, connecting love that would see them through anything. Kyle turned her inside out, upside down and every which way, and Lane couldn't lose her. At least not without a fight. Inhaling the fragrance one more time, Lane replaced the flowers on the table and picked up the phone.

CHAPTER FIFTEEN

Run! Run! Run! Kyle was running and she didn't know where. All she knew was that she had to get away. She couldn't face this. The top was down on her Saab, and the wind whipped her hair as she tore down the highway. Images flashed in front of her as she weaved in and out of traffic, all of them images of Alison. Pictures of their childhood, the tricks twins play on unsuspecting people, Alison graduating from medical school, Alison giving birth. Alison lying motionless in a hospital bed.

No, not again. I can't go through this pain again. I won't go through it again. Kyle wasn't sure if she was thinking about the pain of losing Alison or the possibility of losing Lane.

Slowly she realized that she was unfamiliar with her surroundings. She eased her foot off the gas pedal and directed the car to the side of the road. When she looked around, she had no idea where she was or how long she'd been driving. The terrain was unfamiliar and the sun was burning a trail as it set in the western sky. She looked at her odometer and then her watch. She'd been driving for hours. She started to shake uncontrollably when she realized that she could have very easily killed herself or someone else with her carelessness. She turned off the ignition, put her head in her hands and screamed into the darkness.

Her life had crumbled in a matter of moments. One minute she was reveling in the afterglow of making love to Lane and the next she was shattered. She had never felt for any other woman the way she felt toward Lane. Lane was everything she could ask for, everything she had ever dreamed of in a partner. She was wonderful with Hollie, and Kyle wanted to spend every minute with her.

But her entire universe had changed. One moment they were having a normal conversation, the personal kind lovers shared. The next, her world had disintegrated. The woman who made her happier than anything else with the exception of her daughter was now…what? Kyle couldn't begin to grasp what it meant that Alison's heart was beating inside Lane's chest. The heart that raced under the caresses of her fingers, and the touch of her lips was her sister's. She opened the car door and vomited.

An hour later she pulled back onto the highway in the opposite direction. She drove for thirty-five miles before she was able to determine her location. She pulled into the first gas station she saw and filled her empty tank. While waiting, she opened her cell phone and dialed. After ensuring Hollie's care for the night, she turned her car toward La Jolla. She couldn't go home. She wasn't ready to talk to her parents but there was someone that she could talk to.

❖

Travis grumbled when he looked at the clock. *Jesus Christ, it's nine-thirty.* His angry retort died on his lips when he saw his ravaged partner on his doorstep. "Kyle, what happened?"

As Travis led her into their family room, Kyle tried to find the words to describe how her world had crumbled. Joann was instantly by her side guiding her to the couch. They sat down on either side of her.

Travis spoke first. "Is Hollie okay?" His voice quavered.

She nodded wordlessly and heard him let out a pent up breath.

"What is it? Tell us what happened."

"Lane has Alison's heart." Kyle's voice was flat, devoid of any emotion. She was in shock.

"What?" This time it was Joann who spoke.

"Lane has Alison's heart. She had a heart transplant the same day Alison died."

Joann and Travis exchanged glances. "Kyle, that doesn't mean that she got Alison's heart," Joann said. "It's probably just a coincidence."

Kyle's eyes were dry and her hands were finally still. "Her donor was a young woman who lived back east and died of a brain aneurysm. She received her heart the same day they removed Alison's. Even someone who's not a detective could put two and two together. How many young female donors do you suppose there were that day?" Kyle was suddenly very tired.

"Kyle, where's Hollie?"

"She's with my parents."

"And Lane?"

"I don't know. At her house I guess."

Travis took Kyle's hands and held them tightly. "Kyle, start from the beginning and tell us everything."

Forty-five minutes later, he sat back looking stunned at the chain of events. "Holy Christ. And you're in love with her?"

"I don't know what I feel anymore. I'm just...numb."

"Of course you are," Joann said. "You're in a state of shock."

"I didn't even know she had a heart transplant." Kyle saw the look of disbelief in their eyes. "When we first got together she told me she'd had some surgery on her heart. She called it tinkering, and said that's why she has a scar. She assured me she was fine. I didn't ask a lot of questions. Maybe I should have. I don't know. I was trying to show her some respect. I figured she'd tell me anything else when she was ready."

Travis put his arm around her. "You can't second-guess yourself on this."

Kyle shook her head. "I think I was afraid. It was too close to the pain of losing Alison." She chuckled with bitter irony. "I just had no idea how close. Even after she told me about the transplant, I didn't ask many questions. It brought back too many memories of Alison's death, and I just didn't want to go there again."

Cautiously, Travis said, "I know I said this earlier, but let's not jump to conclusions until we have all the facts. Let me see what I can find out before we assume Alison was involved."

"We can talk about this some more in the morning," Joann eyed Kyle with concern. "You're exhausted. Stay with us tonight and we'll see things clearer in the morning." She gave Kyle a kiss on the cheek. "I'll go make up the guest room."

Kyle lay awake for hours, her mind a whirl of thoughts of the present as well as the past. She relived the pain of having to make the decision to donate her sister's organs. It wasn't something that she and Alison had ever discussed, but Kyle knew it was what her sister would have wanted. Her parents had allowed her to make the decision. She could still feel the pen sliding between her fingers. Her hand had shaken as she signed the consent form. That was the last time she saw Alison.

The burial had been difficult, and executing her will and selling her medical practice was a blur. But nothing was as painful as selling Alison's house. It was several months after the funeral when her mother came with her to sort through Alison's things. Deciding what to keep and what to discard broke her heart into an additional million pieces. Everything she touched brought tears to her eyes. There were so many things she wanted Hollie to have as a reminder of the wonderful woman who was her mother. Kyle packed up far too many things, but she knew someday when Hollie was older she would sort through them again.

Kyle rolled onto her side and let herself weep. The sky had begun to lighten when she finally closed her eyes.

❖

Lane hung up the phone, disappointed. She didn't remember many details about her surgery, and her brother John, while thrilled to hear from her, wasn't able to give her any more information than she already had. Her next call was to her best friend Christina, who was knocking on her door twenty minutes later. They talked long into the night, and every time she retold the events of that afternoon, Lane was still shaken by the fact that she might have Alison's heart. It was late when they finished talking, and Christina spent what was left of the night in Lane's guest room.

Lane woke feeling like she'd been hit by a bus. For a second she thought she was coming down with the flu until she remembered the awful look on Kyle's face. She rolled over in bed and thought about dying, how she almost did and that maybe she wanted to now. She knew that if she had Alison's heart, her relationship with Kyle was over. But she was not going to stand idly by and let Kyle make that decision for both of them. The scent of fresh coffee and the first day of her plan of action drove her out of bed.

Tightening her robe, she entered the kitchen where Christina was pouring each of them a large cup of the hot, strong brew. Christina handed her a cup. "Good morning. I won't ask how you slept. You look like shit."

"Thank you." Lane sat on one of the stools at the counter. She took a few sips of the invigorating coffee while she gathered her thoughts. She was grateful that Christina was her friend. She was supportive of her decision to fight for Kyle but not judgmental of Kyle's reaction. *How did things get so messed up so fast?*

She said as much to Christina, adding, "What did I ever do to deserve any of this?"

"Shit happens, Lane. The question is, what you do with it once it does happen." Christina had always been blunt. "Does it matter whose heart you have?"

Christina's question caught Lane off guard, and she almost spilled her coffee. "Not to me. But it does to Kyle, and I'd probably feel the same if the situation was reversed."

Lane had spent most of the night thinking about how she might be able to determine the name of her donor. Before she finally succumbed to exhaustion, she'd decided to contact her donor representative later that morning. She knew it was a long shot, but she had to do all she could to discover the truth.

"Then I agree with you that you should fight for her. But you know, this is her issue to deal with, not yours."

"How can you say that? I have just as much to deal with as she does. There is a huge possibility that I have the heart of the twin sister of the woman I'm in love with. Other than that being very difficult to say and terribly confusing, don't you think that's just a little creepy?"

"Sweetie, if you think about it too much, *life* is creepy."

"That's a big help."

"I'm just saying I think her pile of shit is bigger than yours. I'm glad you're going to give her some time before you try to talk to her. She needs to deal with this."

"Why are you on her side?"

Christina groaned. "Listen, what you gained, she lost. You

said Hollie looks just like her right?" When Lane nodded, she continued, "Well that's gotta be tough enough and now to believe that her child's mother's heart is beating across the room. I think it's a bit overwhelming."

If Lane weren't so tired she'd be annoyed with Christina's incessant questions and annoying logic. "I couldn't even imagine how that must be. All I know is I can't make her talk about it, and I certainly can't make her get over it. And if that means we never see each other again, I have to respect that. But I'm not going to sit around and do nothing while she makes that decision."

The words sounded noble, but Lane was torn apart as she said them. She wanted to make Kyle believe that it didn't matter whose heart she had. She needed Kyle to believe that she loved her. But she knew she didn't have that kind of power.

❖

Kyle's head throbbed as she drove to her parents' house to pick up Hollie. Joann had forced her to eat a light breakfast, and Travis had assured her he would dig around to see what he could turn up. She felt comforted knowing she had friends as wonderful as these.

When she pulled into the driveway of her parent's house, Hollie was playing in the front yard with her dad. *Oh Hollie, no wonder you connected with her so easily. You knew. Somehow you just knew.*

Seeing her sister's child brought a fresh wave of grief and confusion to her already over-taxed brain. Kyle was afraid that her parents would take one look at her and start asking questions. She put on the best mask she had and got out of the car.

Once she entered the house where she and Alison grew up, memories overwhelmed her. She had to escape or risk breaking down. She felt guilty being abrupt with her father, but she wasn't ready to face her parents with this news. All she wanted was to be alone.

Kyle was relieved that Constance had gone to the grocery store and that she was able to snag Hollie and be back in her car before her father knew what hit him. Hollie chatted nonstop the entire way home, and Kyle exhaled a breath she didn't know she was holding when she turned the corner and saw that Lane's car was not parked in front of her house. She pulled into the garage and quickly closed the door behind her.

Kyle entered the house and her gaze naturally went to the answering machine. One, two, three times the red light winked at her. Moving her focus away from the blinking machine, Kyle picked Hollie up and hugged her tightly.

She spent the rest of the day avoiding the telephone and refusing to clear her messages. As Hollie lay sleeping after a long day of play, Kyle finally moved away from the end of her crib and dragged herself out to the living room. Yet again, she hesitated in front of the machine that had tormented her all day. In one hand she held her third bottle of beer, and the other hand hovered over the play button. The blinking light was not going to go away by itself, and her hand shook as she pushed the button. None of the messages was from Lane.

The phone rang, startling her, and her beer bottle broke when she dropped it on the counter. "Fuck!" Kyle screamed as she cut her finger on a shard of broken glass. The blood splattered on the wall when she pounded her fist on the marble counter. "Goddamn it, son of a bitch!"

Blood dripped on the floor as she slid down the cabinet and fell to the floor. Wrapping a piece of her shirt hem around her finger, she curled up in a fetal position and cried as the machine picked up the call.

"Kyle, it's Travis, and yes I am checking up on you. We're worried about you. I know you're probably going crazy trying to figure this out, but please give it some time. If you need anything, let us know."

Kyle didn't move. It was dark when she opened her eyes again. She had no idea how long she had cried and even less of an idea of how long she'd slept. Her joints were stiff and her left arm had fallen asleep in the awkward position she was in. A stream of light from the full moon blazed through the open curtain. Slowly, she sat up and stretched her legs out in front of her, leaning back against the bar.

"Oh, Allie, what am I going to do? Is your heart in Lane's body or is it just a coincidence? What am I going to tell Mom and Dad? What am I going to tell Hollie when she grows up? Oh God, what am I going to do about Lane?"

Nobody answered back.

A few minutes later, Kyle checked on Hollie, took a hot shower, and climbed into bed. For the second night in a row her dreams were tormented with images of her sister, Hollie, and Lane.

CHAPTER SIXTEEN

D on't look at me like that, Travis. I have a family to support and a job to do. I'm fine."

"Bullshit." Came the one word reply.

Kyle didn't know why she even tried to hide from her partner. He knew her inside and out, and it would be next to impossible to keep anything from him, but it was her natural defense to try. She softened her tone. "Good morning."

"That's better. Good morning, Joann sends her best." He hung his suit jacket on the back of his chair and sat down.

"Thank her for me," Kyle said.

She knew her friends would have been talking about her ever since she showed up on their doorstep and were worrying about how she was handling the stress of the whole situation. They knew how close she'd been to Alison, and she'd made the mistake of sharing her feelings about Lane. They probably thought she was going over the deep end, but her head was clearer this morning than it had been all weekend even if her natural ability to reason had not yet returned.

"Travis, I know you mean well, but I can't talk about it right now. There is so much going through my head I can't think straight, and I have to get back on an even keel. I need to work to get my mind off it for a while." She reached across the desk and touched his hand. "You know I love you guys and when I'm ready I'll talk about it. Okay?"

Travis eyed her critically. "I'm going to say three things then I promise I'll shut up. First, you have to talk to someone about this, a counselor or somebody who has the expertise to help you figure this all out. Second," he ticked off the number on his fingers, "I'm going to keep digging around and see what I can turn up. And third, go talk to Lane. I can see what's going on between you two, and she has to be in as much shock about all of this as you are. It's not her fault. Oh, by the way, Joann wants you and Hollie to come to dinner some night this week." He sat back in his chair, his comments complete.

"That was more than three things," Kyle said teasingly trying to regain her lost sense of humor. She held up her fingers as she replied. "One, I'll think about it. Two, you probably won't get far, but thanks. Three, I can't, at least not yet, and four, how about Wednesday? I'll try to be social by then."

Before her partner had a chance to reply, Kyle's phone rang and another day in the Homicide Division of the La Jolla Police Department began.

❖

"I'm sorry, what did you say?" Lane looked past Donna toward the front door hoping that it was Kyle that just walked in instead of the two business men.

She knew Kyle wouldn't come into the restaurant, but she couldn't stop scanning the faces of her customers each time she ventured out onto the patio. For two hours, Kyle's normal table had remained empty until Lane herself sat a customer there. Donna noticed her pensive mood and had smartly avoided approaching her with anything serious until now.

Lane had spent the better part of yesterday talking to her transplant coordinator and scouring the Internet for anything she could find on Alison Bain. The coordinator had provided her with no information whatsoever, citing program confidentiality. But the Internet offered a wealth of information. The more Lane read about Alison the more she recognized so much of Kyle in her. They were both dynamic, strong women, passionate about people and their work. There were several pictures of the two of them together, and the resemblance was remarkable. Lane read between the lines and saw the love and devotion they had for each other.

The obituary for Alison was short and brief, but the tributes by her patients and fellow physicians were numerous. Colleagues from around the country spoke of Alison's intelligence and compassion for her patients, saying that the medical community had lost a great individual when she died. Lane found a copy of Alison's will that had been filed upon her death, naming Kyle as executor of her estate and the guardian of her child. Property and insurance records indicated that Kyle was the sole beneficiary of her estate and that she'd established a significant trust fund for Hollie. The documents also indicated that Kyle had received enough money that she didn't need to work for the rest of her life.

That Kyle had chosen to juggle the demands of motherhood and work in order to bring murderers to justice only made Lane respect her all the more.

Oh Kyle, what you must be going through.

❖

"Kyle, is something troubling you?" For the past several weeks Constance had suspected that her daughter was putting up a good front for their benefit.

Kyle held her breath as she looked up from the cutting board where she had been concentrating on cubing a block of cheese. "What do you mean?"

Keep calm. Keep your face neutral. You can do this.

Her mother gave her the look that told Kyle that she knew she'd been caught. "I'm waiting."

"I'm trying to work out a few issues. Nothing serious."

Constance saw right through her. "You could never lie to me when you were a little girl, and you still can't even though you're a grown woman."

How does she do that?

"Is it a case you're working on?"

"No." *Shit, why did I say that? I could have used it as an excuse.*

"Then what is it, darling? Even your father can tell something's bothering you. You've lost weight and you look tired. I hardly ever see you smile unless you're with Hollie, and then it looks like you're holding on to her for dear life."

Kyle shrugged. She hadn't realized she'd been losing weight, but now that she thought about it, all her clothes felt loose. Sleep only came when she was totally exhausted, and the old nightmares of the fire had returned. She often woke in the middle of the night unable, or unwilling, to fall back asleep. She tried to eat, but everything tasted like chalk and got stuck in her throat. Her mother was right about how she was with Hollie. At first her daughter had basked in the extra attention, but these days she scrambled off Kyle's lap as often as she could.

Kyle glanced out the window. Her father had taken Hollie outside, and they were both laughing as he pushed her on the swing. "I don't really want to talk about it, Mom."

"Is there anything I can do?"

Her mother had always been there for her, and they both needed each other more than ever when Alison died. Suddenly Kyle couldn't keep it bottled up inside anymore. "It involves Lane." She didn't get to finish her explanation before her mother spoke up.

"Has she done something to hurt you?" No matter how old a child was it was still a mother's instinct to protect her offspring, and Kyle recognized the familiar warning note in her voice.

"No, Mom. At least not directly." Kyle put the knife down and searched her mother's eyes. What she found there gave her the courage to continue. "Last March Lane had a heart transplant. When we first starting seeing each other I didn't know and when she told me I didn't ask too many questions. I guess it brought up too many memories of Alison." Kyle saw the momentary flicker of grief cross her mother's face and then it was gone.

"To cut a long story short, it seems there's a high probability that she received Alison's heart."

"What? How can that be? It's all confidential. The names of donors are never released."

"She doesn't know the name of her donor, but the specifics mirror Alison's right down to the date and the cause of death. Needless to say it's a bit unnerving."

"When did you learn about this?" Constance's tone was stern and Kyle had no other choice but to answer.

"Almost three weeks ago."

"And you didn't say anything?" Constance began pacing around the kitchen. "Kyle, how could you keep this from us?"

"I didn't want you and Dad to go through this." Kyle tried to explain.

"Were you intending to keep it a secret forever?" Constance looked angry and hurt.

"I don't know. I don't know anything anymore." Kyle's

frustration and confusion broke through, and her reply was harsher than she had expected. She slammed the knife on the counter. "I've been trying to figure it out. Jesus Christ, Mom, give me a break. I've been sleeping with the woman who has my sister's heart! What the fuck am I supposed to do with that?"

Constance stared at her for several moments before Kyle lowered her head. Finally able to put into words the anguish she had been experiencing for weeks, she said, "I don't know whether to rejoice because a part of Allie is still alive or throw up because I'm making love to it." Her mother finally seemed to realize the pain she was in and came around the counter and pulled her into her arms. They moved through the kitchen and into the living room and sat down next to each other on the couch. Kyle held her mother's hand like it was a lifeline.

"We were seeing a lot of each other. We'd get together several times a week, and on the weekends we'd do something with Hollie. Hollie loved her. Their instant connection makes perfect sense now."

"Are you in love with her?"

Kyle looked up in surprise at her mother's question. "I don't know. A few weeks ago I might have said yes. Now it's just not that simple anymore."

"What does she say?"

"I haven't talked to her since I found out."

"Yes, I suppose that would be difficult." Her mother frowned as if she was still absorbing the full meaning of the information. "I'm so sorry, darling. To believe that the heart of someone you loved more than anything is in the body of the woman you love… that's truly shocking."

"Travis thinks it might just be a coincidence. He's trying to dig up information about Lane's transplant to see if he can tie the two together."

"And if he does?"

"I don't know."

"What can I do to help you with this, Kyle?"

Kyle knew that if she was going through hell, her parents would be as well. "You've got enough to deal with now that you know. I don't want to add to it."

"Nonsense. We need to be together as a family during this, whatever the outcome."

And a closer family they became. They had dinner together at least three or four nights a week, and several times Kyle spent the night in their guest room. It was only on those nights that the nightmares stayed away and she was able to get a full night's sleep. Her parents watched her like a hawk when they were together, looking for any signs of how they could help her weather this storm. But they didn't tell her what they thought she should do. Kyle was thankful for that. Her parents understood her well enough to know this was something she had to maneuver through alone.

❖

One more mile. I can do this. I feel good. I need this. Lane concentrated on her breathing and her heart rate, ignoring the burning in her legs. Her stamina was increasing, and she was rediscovering her love of mountain biking. Riding was when she was the most at peace. The strenuous physical exertion and concentration required to stay upright barreling down a hill at twenty miles an hour left room for little else to fill her head. Today however, no amount of speed or challenging terrain could drive Kyle out of her mind.

Lane released her grip from the handlebars and wiped the sweat that dripped off her brow. Her helmet was ventilated but had very little actual cooling effect. As she rode, she replayed the scene in her mind when Kyle learned the details of her surgery. The expression on Kyle's face was burned indelibly into her brain. She saw it when she closed her eyes at night and whenever she thought about Kyle at work or anywhere else. And now, when she was trying to do something for herself, she saw it again, right in front of her.

Shit! One minute she was descending an intermediate slope and the next she was sprawled in a heap in the dirt. Her lack of concentration meant she didn't notice the trail had more sand on it than usual. Her front tire hit the sand as if it was thick mud, and she was catapulted over the handlebars. Spitting sand from her mouth, Lane cautiously moved each of her extremities. To her relief nothing appeared to be broken. The last time she took a spill like this she broke her collar bone in two places. Grateful that she only suffered a few minor scrapes she dusted off the evidence of her fall and climbed back onto the saddle.

Lane, fresh from a shower and sporting a large bandage on her right elbow, was distracted as she drove into the restaurant parking lot. She didn't notice the dark green Chevrolet Caprice parked down the street, and as she got out, the wind blew her hair into her face. She pushed the strands away from her eyes with one hand and pulled open the front door of The SandPiper with the other.

A few minutes later, when she was sitting behind the desk in her office, someone knocked.

"Come in," Lane replied.

Over the past month or so she'd been spending more and more time in her office, finding it difficult to put on a welcoming face for her customers. She didn't look up until she heard the door open, and when she did, her eyes traced a path from the polished shoes, up the creased trousers, past the badge and gun, over a firm chest and smooth jaw stopping at a pair of strong brown eyes.

"Good morning, Detective. Is this business or a social call?"

"Both. Can we talk?"

Lane indicated the chair in front of her desk. Seeing the detective in her office made her heart ache. She remained cautious until she knew exactly where the conversation was headed. She didn't have to wait long.

"How are you, Lane?" The voice was smooth and husky.

"I've been better."

"You look tired. Are you taking care of yourself?"

The lines of tension on Lane's face were obvious to her, so they wouldn't escape the detective's trained eye. She didn't bother to pretend she felt great. "As best as can be expected."

"Yes, I suppose that's true." The occupant in the chair sighed deeply and was obviously troubled.

"Why are you here, Travis?"

"Kyle told me what happened between you two. I'm sorry."

"How is she?" Lane choked out the question through a dry throat.

The smile on Travis' face was usually mistaken as a smirk. "About the same as you. Shitty." He continued before Lane had a chance to say anything. "Lane, I'm a detective, someone who searches for the facts and uncovers the truth. I don't believe in coincidences."

"And?" Lane wasn't sure where he was going with this.

"It almost killed Kyle when Alison died. They were kindred spirits. I remember one time we were walking to get some lunch when Kyle stumbled. There was absolutely nothing on the ground, and she said that she had felt a jarring pain shoot up her leg just before she stumbled. The pain lasted all afternoon, and she came to find out that was the day and the exact time Alison broke her leg skiing."

"And you've come to me for?" Lane still didn't know why Kyle's partner was here sharing history she didn't want to hear about. But one thing was certain. If he had verification of the connection between her and Alison, she would lose Kyle forever. *Who am I kidding? I've already lost her.*

"I have to help her, Lane. I've gone as far as I can to try to track this down, and I need some information from you. Your surgery, blood type, doctors, that sort of thing."

Lane leaned back in her chair and steepled her fingers under her chin. "You know, if I give you the information, and you find out the truth, there's a good chance I'll never see Kyle again."

"The same applies if you don't. In my book that qualifies as a no-win situation." Travis ran his fingers through his thick dark hair. "Look, the only chance you have for her to come back to you is to confirm that the heart you have is not Alison's. And the only way that'll happen is for you to answer a few questions."

The tension in the room was palpable. Lane could sense Travis was as afraid of the answers as she was, whatever they might be.

"What do you know so far?" she asked.

Travis didn't answer right away.

"Travis, possession is nine tenths of the law, and since the heart in question is sutured into my chest I get the most votes in this game."

Reluctantly, he said, "There were two thirty-five-year-old women who died from a brain aneurysm on March 24th. One lived in North Carolina and Alison lived in Connecticut. The families of both women donated their organs. Both hearts were transplanted. Unfortunately, I don't know which one you received."

"But you intend to find out?"

"I think Kyle has a right to know."

This was one of those moments that defined an individual. Or was it one of those times that the character of the individual defined the moment? Lane's decision could affect the lives of dozens of people, and that knowledge was humbling.

Do I want to know? Can I handle it if I know? Will it make any difference in my life if I know? All of these questions had been coursing through her mind for weeks, and she was no closer to the answers than on the first day. She thought of Kyle and of the dream she'd once had for their life together, a dream she still hadn't let go of entirely. She had promised herself she would fight for Kyle, and she needed every weapon she could find.

Taking a deep breath, she said, "I think we both have a right to know. What do you need from me?"

CHAPTER SEVENTEEN

K yle knocked on the door of apartment 212, glancing at her watch. It was just after midnight and she knew she'd be unable to sleep. Her head was filled with images of a tiny child battered almost beyond recognition. Abigail Marie Stensen was dead. Preliminary investigation revealed that the little girl had suffered from horrific abuse during her short life, and her mother's boyfriend had finally thrown one punch too many. Kyle had had a bad feeling about the call, and when she rounded the corner, the flashing lights from two fire trucks and four police cruisers indicated the severity of the case. Captain Grainger had assigned Kyle due to her high conviction rate with homicides involving children, and he knew this particular case would be difficult since the prime suspect was a district attorney's nephew.

Sick at heart, Kyle leaned against the wall as she waited for the occupant to unlock the door. *What am I doing here?*

She was in the same spot now as she had been the first time she and Stephanie got together. On that evening, after yet another horrible scene witnessing what one human was capable of doing to another, she had found herself on Stephanie's doorstep. Neither of them was looking for a commitment, but they both needed an outlet. They didn't fall in love, or even in lust. They were simply two people who didn't make judgments about how they coped with the unique stresses they faced. Kyle almost fell in the door when it opened. No words were spoken as Stephanie gathered her into her arms. Theirs was a mutual need as they were both involved with Abigail's death. Stephanie had been a first responder to that gruesome scene. She had given up on trying to sleep and was sitting in front of the TV when Kyle arrived. As they walked toward the bedroom she didn't ask why Kyle was there nor did she care. All she knew was that they shared a profession that was dangerous, thrilling and often times ugly, and they understood each other as very few others did.

Kyle had struggled with her decision to come to Stephanie, torn between the need to escape and the desire to be with the woman she loved. In the end she took the easy, predictable way out, and now here she was in the arms of a desirable woman feeling guilty. Guilty for being here in the first place and guilty for using Stephanie.

"Shh, it's all right. You've got every right to be wound up tighter than a guitar string. Just relax."

"That poor child." Kyle ran her hands through her hair. "I'm going to nail the cowardly bastard that beat her to death if it's the last thing I do. God, Steph, it was the worst I've ever seen." Kyle shuddered. "And tomorrow is the autopsy. All I can see is that little girl cut open on the table. Children should *never* be on an autopsy table."

"I know. But you have to find some comfort in the fact that you're going to make sure that animal will never get the opportunity to hurt another child."

"That helps. But sometimes it's just not enough."

Stephanie broke away and led them toward the bedroom. Kyle tensed when Stephanie pulled her onto the bed.

"Easy girl, I'm not going anywhere," Stephanie murmured against her neck.

The words meant nothing to Kyle. She needed to escape.

She needed to get lost in something, anything. Her mind had not stopped racing since the news of Alison's heart in Lane's body. She couldn't concentrate, she snapped at everybody, and even her time with Hollie was different. The more she tried not to think about Lane, the more everything reminded her of something they had done together or that Kyle wanted to do with her. Her life was in a tailspin.

Kyle rolled Stephanie onto her back and got rid of the robe and pajama top in one motion. She couldn't be the passive one this time, she had to take control. She hoped the familiarity of reaching out to Stephanie would help get her life back on track.

Kyle froze when Stephanie's full breast filled her hand. The weight felt foreign. Instead of being familiar, it felt like it didn't belong. The texture was different, the size too large, and the erect nipple was not the one that she yearned to tease with her tongue. Kyle shuddered, rolled off Stephanie and lay on her back, staring up at the ceiling.

"Kyle?"

"I can't do this. I... shouldn't be here." Kyle needed comfort but the instant Stephanie was in her arms, she knew she was with the wrong woman.

"I was wondering why you hadn't come around in months. You seem different somehow. Does this have anything to do with the woman you were with at the restaurant?" Stephanie got out of bed and gathered her robe around her.

"It's complicated."

"It always is."

"You don't even know the half of it." Kyle got off the bed and crossed to the door. "I'm sorry Stephanie, I've gotta go. I never should have come here in the first place."

There was only one woman she wanted comfort from. One woman who made her strong enough to be vulnerable. One woman who reached through her and touched her heart. And whether she could deal with it or not, that woman was Lane.

"You know you're always welcome here, Kyle."

Kyle smiled. "You're a good friend."

"Take care of yourself. And whatever the complication is, work through it."

Kyle leaned down and placed a soft chaste kiss on Stephanie's lips. "Thanks. I'm trying to."

❖

The morning of Abigail Stensen's funeral, Kyle found herself in a familiar location with a comforting view. The beautiful scenery notwithstanding, her stomach was in knots and her heart raced at the sight of the woman across the patio. The funeral was going to be difficult, and Kyle had spent the last three days preparing herself. She didn't know why she'd come to The SandPiper this morning; she'd simply acted on the desire to be here. She held her breath when Lane turned around.

Lane froze in her tracks at the sight of her detective. Kyle was even more stunning than she remembered, and the intensity of her gaze was almost unbearable. She waited for some sign from Kyle to indicate that her presence was welcome. Kyle gave her a small smile. Lane swallowed hard and prayed that one foot would move in front of the other.

Kyle took in every inch of the woman walking toward her and noticed that Lane looked thinner and the sparkle in her eyes was gone. "Hello, Lane."

"Kyle." Lane managed to squeak out over suddenly dry lips. *What are you doing here?*

"Do you have a minute?"

For Kyle, she had a lifetime. "Certainly." Lane held her breath as she sat down.

"How have you been?" Kyle flinched inwardly at her inquiry of Lane's health. She clearly remembered Lane didn't want to be treated differently because of her illness.

"I'm well. And you?" Lane knew she looked like hell but would never admit it.

"I'm fine. You look tired." *This conversation is going nowhere.*

"Just busy." *Say something! Talk to me! Tell me that you love me and need me regardless of whose heart I have. I'm offering it to you!*

Kyle turned the coffee cup in her hands as she looked into the dark liquid for words. What she saw instead was a dark abyss that mirrored the way she felt, a future unclear and uncertain. Her eyes shifted between Lane's and the place on Lane's chest where she knew a strong heart beat.

Lane saw the struggle on Kyle's face, and her heart broke even further. Kyle was here and Lane didn't know if she wanted to hear what she had to say. As she felt her heart pound, she made a decision.

"Kyle, I don't know why you're here, but I want to say something." She took a deep breath and squared her shoulders. "I care about you and I can't let this go without a fight."

"We can't talk now," Kyle said softly. "I have to go very soon."

"You can give me five minutes." Lane challenged her with a stare that left no room for argument. "I think I'm owed that."

Kyle didn't respond.

"This has been a shock to both of us, and I won't even begin to say I can imagine what you're going through, because I can't. But, Kyle, you're a detective, and I would have expected you to need more concrete evidence before you jumped to a conclusion. Especially one that has as much of an impact on your life as this.

"Kyle, I love you. We had something special between us. I felt warm and protected when I was with you, and I can't even describe how I felt to be in your arms. I've never experienced what I feel when I'm with you. We were good together, and I think Hollie liked me. She certainly had become an important part of my life. I could see the possibility of a future with you. You can't tell me that you didn't feel something too. I *know* you did. I could see it in your eyes, and I could feel it when you touched me. We had all of that, before you found out about the transplant."

Kyle didn't give any indication that she was going to say anything, so Lane continued. "A heart is just a pump, Kyle. It's an organ that does something specific for the body. It doesn't make a person who they are. It has nothing to do with who they are. That's determined by their parents, their upbringing, the people they hang around with, and who they love. My heart does not define who I am. I didn't become a different person when I got a new one. I'm the same person I was before I got sick, and I'm the same person that I was before you found out. The only thing about me that's different is *a part*, a simple yet complex part. I'm just grateful to be alive, and I want you and Hollie to be a part of my life."

Lane sat back in her chair. She knew that she had given a great deal of thought to how she felt, and she hoped that she was articulate enough to get her point across.

Kyle sat motionless, her mind numb with the words and feelings expressed by the woman who was sitting so close to her. She longed to reach out and hold Lane's hand, the one that was so strong yet so soft, but she couldn't. She was ashamed that she felt the way she did. Lane had moved on with her life, why couldn't she? *Because it was my sister.*

When it was apparent that Kyle was not going to comment,

Lane stood. Kyle rose as she always did, and her body screamed to close the distance between them. "I hope to see you again, Kyle."

She took one last look in the dark eyes that had once been filled with desire and now haunted her dreams, then turned and walked away.

❖

Later that afternoon, Kyle eagerly arrested the murderer of Abigail Stensen. When she snapped the handcuffs she was silently disappointed he didn't put up a fight. She wasn't the only cop waiting for the smallest excuse to beat the shit out of him. She was finishing up the intake paperwork when Travis returned with two sandwiches for their dinner.

"Have you talked to Lane yet?" he asked

Kyle's fingers momentarily froze over the keyboard before she returned to pecking at the keys. "Yes, I saw her this morning."

"And?"

"She did most of the talking."

"What did she say?"

Kyle gave up on trying to concentrate on the report. She pushed the keyboard tray away and turned to face her partner. "Some interesting things."

"Like what?"

"Like a heart is just a pump, just a piece of machinery. It doesn't define who you are, and she's the same person she was before she got sick and before I found out about it. She said she was disappointed in me that I jumped to conclusions and didn't wait for confirmation."

"Whoa, that's pretty heavy stuff."

"Not nearly as heavy as when she told me that she loves me." Kyle's voice dropped to almost a whisper. A whisper seemed to be the right tone of voice to repeat the words that Lane had confessed to her earlier.

"And you said?" Travis asked expectantly.

Kyle lowered her eyes. "Nothing."

"Nothing? The woman tells you she loves you and you say nothing? Even a dope like me knows that's a really big deal."

"Travis shut up! I'm not made of stone and I'm certainly not perfect. The woman has my sister's heart beating inside of her. The heart I can hear pounding in the middle of the night when I lay my head on her shoulder. The heart that races when I touch her and is breaking because I can't deal with this. Travis, you're like a brother to me, but please give me a fucking break."

❖

The break that Kyle received was not what she had asked for nor was it what she expected. It happened three days later and was a break of the radius bone in her left arm. She and Travis were interviewing a suspect in his living room and in one moment he went from calm and cooperative to swinging a Louisville Slugger in her direction. Travis successfully subdued the man, but only after Kyle's arm had been broken in two places.

It was the white cast that Lane noticed first about her detective. *She's not my detective anymore.* "Should I ask what the other guy looks like?"

"About six-five, brown hair, lots of tattoos and twelve stitches in his head." Kyle held the chair for her to sit.

"I take it that you won?"

Kyle couldn't take her eyes off the woman seated next to her. It felt good to be sitting on the patio of The SandPiper again.

"I'm the good guy, he was the bad guy. I always win." She smiled at the easy way her replies came to mind. *God I miss her.*

"I saw you on the news the other night talking about the murder of that little girl." Lane saw a flash of pain cross Kyle's face before she could mask it. "That must have been very difficult for you. Are you okay?"

Kyle knew that Lane was referring to the nightmares she experienced when investigating a case involving children. Kyle was tired. She didn't want to try to convince Lane of something that wasn't true.

"I have my moments. But I'm okay."

The anguish that appeared on Kyle's face tore at Lane's heart. As much as she wanted to speak, she forced herself to sit back and listen. Kyle wouldn't be here unless she had something to say.

"It almost killed me when Allie died," Kyle said abruptly. "It was like losing a part of me, the best part. She was everything to me, and I wanted to die with her. But I couldn't. She'd given me the privilege of raising her child, and I couldn't let her down. I *won't* let her down." Kyle's voice was strong in conviction, but as her eyes dropped to the table Lane glimpsed a trace of shame in their depths. "But I can't deal with this. Maybe I'm shallow, or maybe I'm overly sensitive, but right now when I look at you all I see is my sister's face and I can't do it. If you get sick or your body rejects the heart, I can't go through that again. I can't lose her again. I'm sorry."

Lane remained calm even though she wanted to scream. "Kyle, do you know for a fact that this heart is Alison's?"

Kyle shook her head.

"Then don't sell us short until you do. Yes, I'm going to die, we all are. For crying out loud, you're a cop! You have a higher probability of dying than I do." Lane sighed leaning forward

CHAPTER EIGHTEEN

It was a warm spring day, and Hollie was enjoying it as only a two-year-old can. She sat on her mother's lap smelling the flowers she held in her chubby little hands.

"Hollie, put them over there." Kyle indicated the spot where the flowers were to go.

Her daughter proudly did as she was told and then ran into the arms of her grandmother standing several yards away. Kyle watched her parents and daughter walk back toward the car. They were here to commemorate the second anniversary of Alison's death. Five days earlier they'd celebrated Hollie's birthday.

"Allie, can you see your little girl? She looks so much like you, and Mom says she's the spitting image of you at her age. She's a good girl, and I know you'd be proud of her. I'm doing the best I know how to raise her. Thank you for giving me this honor. I promise, Hollie will always know you're her mama. God, I miss you."

Kyle plucked a few blades of grass and let them slip through her fingers. "I've met someone, Al. You'd really like her. Hollie's crazy about her. And I am too. Her name is Lane and she's absolutely charming. She is a wonderful, kind woman and she willingly puts up with my job, my schedule, and our child. She takes my breath away just to look at her, Al, and my body cries out to touch her."

Kyle didn't care what others thought of her as she talked to her sister's headstone. "There's only one problem. I think she has your heart. Yeah, sounds crazy doesn't it. Believe me I've been trying to figure it out for months now. It's been kind of creepy thinking that the woman you had sex with might have your sister's heart. Jesus this sounds like a soap opera."

"All the evidence points to one conclusion, except this one thing." She held up a sealed white envelope. "Travis gave me this before I left. He called it the smoking gun. It proves one way or the other if it's your heart."

Kyle had been with him when the fax came across the wire. He had been beside her with his unspoken support as she sifted through reports, newspaper archives, and medical journals searching for the answer she needed. When the final piece arrived, she wasn't sure she was ready. She asked him to take the paper and seal it in an envelope.

"I haven't opened it, Al. I don't know if I want to know what's inside. I love her, but I don't think I could be with her if it's your heart." Her hands shook and the tears flowed unabashed down her cheeks. "But I don't know if I can live without her. Oh Allie, please help me, please tell me what to do."

❖

Lane thought she was doing a good job of faking it. That is until Christina came up beside her. "You really don't want any part of this do you?"

Lane looked around the restaurant at all of her friends and family that had gathered to celebrate the second anniversary of her life. She should be thrilled that she was healthy and surrounded by people that loved her. She leaned into Christina's arm around her shoulder. "Not this year, no."

"Thanks for indulging us." Christina hesitated before asking, "Have you spoken to her lately?"

Lane didn't need to pretend that she didn't know who *she* was. "No. She hasn't been in."

"I still think you need to go get her."

"Christina, I know you mean well, but I can't. She needs to come to me. This is her issue to resolve, not mine."

And that was the most frustrating part. Lane was a woman of action and having no control over this situation made her feel absolutely helpless.

"Come on," Christina said. "I think they're cutting the cake without you."

Lane sat alone in her office, her shoes off and her feet on the table. She wanted to unwind before heading home. The front door opened and she assumed it was one of the custodial crew cleaning up after the party. A movement in the corner of her eye drew her attention to the doorway.

"I hope I'm not disturbing you. I saw the lights on and took a chance." Kyle was nervous, shifting her weight from foot to foot.

Lane reeled in her heart. "No not at all. Come in. Can I get you something?"

Kyle came into the office but didn't sit down. "No thanks I had something on the plane."

"The plane?"

"My parents and I took Hollie to Alison's grave. I guess I don't have to tell you why." Kyle walked slowly around the small room picking up little knick-knacks Lane had placed around her office.

"No." This time Lane would let Kyle do the talking.

"She's really too young, but it's something I think is important." Kyle stopped and sat down on the table in front of Lane. "Before I left, Travis gave me this." She held up the envelope. It was no longer pristine white and stiff. She had held it too tightly for too long in the hope that she would eventually know the right thing to do with it.

"What is it?"

"The last piece of information that will prove whether or not you have Allie's heart." Kyle's tone seemed harsh, but they were way past the point of beating around the bush.

Lane struggled to remain calm. The envelope was unopened. "What are you going to do with it?"

"I asked Allie the same question. She didn't answer me. One of the few times my sister had nothing to say and I needed her the most." Kyle smiled fondly. "It's pretty apparent this is my decision to make."

"And have you?" Lane held her breath. Kyle's next words would either tear her world apart permanently or cause the sun to shine again.

"Yes." Kyle's eyes had always been the window to her soul, but this time there was an intensity that Lane did not recognize. Her gaze drilled right down to Lane's core.

Kyle rose and walked over to the corner of Lane's desk. She held the envelope in both hands, studied it one more time, then dropped it in the paper shredder.

"It doesn't matter whose heart you have, Lane. I'm just thankful that you got one. Because if you hadn't, then I wouldn't be loved by someone so wonderful." Kyle returned to her place in front of Lane and took both of her hands in hers. "I wouldn't be able to say that I love you. I wouldn't be able to tell you that you are the most important person in my life and that I want to spend the rest of my life with you. I want you to help me raise Hollie. I love you Lane. How could I have ever doubted it?"

Lane put her finger to the lips that drove her crazy and were responsible for passionate delights like she had never known. They were as soft and warm as she remembered. "Ssh. What matters is that we're together now."

Kyle's eyes were explosive with love and passion that would last a lifetime. Lane cupped Kyle's face in her hands and kissed her gently.

"Let's go home."

About the Author

Julie Cannon is a native sun goddess born and raised in Phoenix, Arizona. After a five year stint in "snow up to my #$&" and temperatures that hovered in the 30's, she returned to the Valley of the Sun vowing never to leave again. Julie's day job is in Corporate America, and her nights are spent bringing to life the stories that bounce around in her head throughout the day.

Julie and her partner, Laura, have been together for sixteen years and spend their weekends camping, riding ATV's, or lounging around the pool with their seven-year-old son and daughter.

Books Available From Bold Strokes Books

Place of Exile by Rose Beecham. Sheriff's detective Jude Devine struggles with ghosts of her past and an ex-lover who still haunts her dreams. (978-1-933110-98-1)

Fully Involved by Erin Dutton. A love that has smoldered for years ignites when two women and one little boy come together in the aftermath of tragedy. (978-1-933110-99-8)

Heart 2 Heart by Julie Cannon. Suffering from a devastating personal loss, Kyle Bain meets Lane Connor, and the chance for happiness suddenly seems possible. (978-1-60282-000-5)

Queens of Tristaine: Tristaine Book Four by Cate Culpepper. When a deadly plague stalks the Amazons of Tristaine, two warrior lovers must return to the place of their nightmares to find a cure. (978-1-933110-97-4)

The Crown of Valencia by Catherine Friend. Ex-lovers can really mess up your life…even, as Kate discovers, if they've traveled back to the 11th century! (978-1-933110-96-7)

Mine by Georgia Beers. What happens when you've already given your heart and love finds you again? Courtney McAllister is about to find out. (978-1-933110-95-0)

House of Clouds by KI Thompson. A sweeping saga of an impassioned romance between a Northern spy and a Southern sympathizer, set amidst the upheaval of a nation under siege. (978-1-933110-94-3)

Winds of Fortune by Radclyffe. Provincetown local Deo Camara agrees to rehab Dr. Nita Burgoyne's historic home, but she never said anything about mending her heart. (978-1-933110-93-6)

Focus of Desire by Kim Baldwin. Isabel Sterling is surprised when she wins a photography contest, but no more than photographer Natasha Kashnikova. Their promo tour becomes a ticket to romance. (978-1-933110-92-9)

Blind Leap by Diane and Jacob Anderson-Minshall. A Golden Gate Bridge suicide becomes suspect when a filmmaker's camera shows a different story. Yoshi Yakamota and the Blind Eye Detective Agency uncover evidence that could be worth killing for. (978-1-933110-91-2)

Wall of Silence, 2nd ed. by Gabrielle Goldsby. Life takes a dangerous turn when jaded police detective Foster Everett meets Riley Medeiros, a woman who isn't afraid to discover the truth no matter the cost. (978-1-933110-90-5)

Mistress of the Runes by Andrews & Austin. Passion ignites between two women with ties to ancient secrets, contemporary mysteries, and a shared quest for the meaning of life. (978-1-933110-89-9)

Sheridan's Fate by Gun Brooke. A dynamic, erotic romance between physical therapist Lark Mitchell and businesswoman Sheridan Ward set in the scorching hot days and humid, steamy nights of San Antonio. (978-1-933110-88-2)

Vulture's Kiss by Justine Saracen. Archeologist Valerie Foret, heir to a terrifying task, returns in a powerful desert adventure set in Egypt and Jerusalem. (978-1-933110-87-5)

Rising Storm by JLee Meyer. The sequel to *First Instinct* takes our heroines on a dangerous journey instead of the honeymoon they'd planned. (978-1-933110-86-8)

Not Single Enough by Grace Lennox. A funny, sexy modern romance about two lonely women who bond over the unexpected and fall in love along the way. (978-1-933110-85-1)

Such a Pretty Face by Gabrielle Goldsby. A sexy, sometimes humorous, sometimes biting contemporary romance that gently exposes the damage to heart and soul when we fail to look beneath the surface for what truly matters. (978-1-933110-84-4)

Second Season by Ali Vali. A romance set in New Orleans amidst betrayal, Hurricane Katrina, and the new beginnings hardship and heartbreak sometimes make possible. (978-1-933110-83-7)

Hearts Aflame by Ronica Black. A poignant, erotic romance between a hard-driving businesswoman and a solitary vet. Packed with adventure and set in the harsh beauty of the Arizona countryside. (978-1-933110-82-0)

Red Light by JD Glass. Tori forges her path as an EMT in the New York City 911 system while discovering what matters most to herself and the woman she loves. (978-1-933110-81-3)

Honor Under Siege by Radclyffe. Secret Service agent Cameron Roberts struggles to protect her lover while searching for a traitor who just may be another woman with a claim on her heart. (978-1-933110-80-6)

Dark Valentine by Jennifer Fulton. Danger and desire fuel a high stakes cat-and-mouse game when an attorney and an endangered witness team up to thwart a killer. (978-1-933110-79-0)

Sequestered Hearts by Erin Dutton. A popular artist suddenly goes into seclusion; a reluctant reporter wants to know why; and a heart locked away yearns to be set free. (978-1-933110-78-3)

Erotic Interludes 5: *Road Games* eds. Radclyffe and Stacia Seaman. Adventure, "sport," and sex on the road—hot stories of travel adventures and games of seduction. (978-1-933110-77-6)

The Spanish Pearl by Catherine Friend. On a trip to Spain, Kate Vincent is accidentally transported back in time...an epic saga spiced with humor, lust, and danger. (978-1-933110-76-9)

Lady Knight by L-J Baker. Loyalty and honour clash with love and ambition in a medieval world of magic when female knight Riannon meets Lady Eleanor. (978-1-933110-75-2)

Dark Dreamer by Jennifer Fulton. Best-selling horror author, Rowe Devlin falls under the spell of psychic Phoebe Temple. A Dark Vista romance. (978-1-933110-74-5)

Come and Get Me by Julie Cannon. Elliott Foster isn't used to pursuing women, but alluring attorney Lauren Collier makes her change her mind. (978-1-933110-73-8)

Blind Curves by Diane and Jacob Anderson-Minshall. Private eye Yoshi Yakamota comes to the aid of her ex-lover Velvet Erickson in the first Blind Eye mystery. (978-1-933110-72-1)

Dynasty of Rogues by Jane Fletcher. It's hate at first sight for Ranger Riki Sadiq and her new patrol corporal, Tanya Coppelli—except for their undeniable attraction. (978-1-933110-71-4)

Running With the Wind by Nell Stark. Sailing instructor Corrie Marsten has signed off on love until she meets Quinn Davies—one woman she can't ignore. (978-1-933110-70-7)

More than Paradise by Jennifer Fulton. Two women battle danger, risk all, and find in one another an unexpected ally and an unforgettable love. (978-1-933110-69-1)

Flight Risk by Kim Baldwin. For Blayne Keller, being in the wrong place at the wrong time just might turn out to be the best thing that ever happened to her. (978-1-933110-68-4)

Rebel's Quest, Supreme Constellations Book Two by Gun Brooke. On a world torn by war, two women discover a love that defies all boundaries. (978-1-933110-67-7)

Punk and Zen by JD Glass. Angst, sex, love, rock. Trace, Candace, Francesca...Samantha. Losing control—and finding the truth within. BSB Victory Editions. (1-933110-66-X)

Stellium in Scorpio by Andrews & Austin. The passionate reuniting of two powerful women on the glitzy Las Vegas Strip where everything is an illusion and love is a gamble. (1-933110-65-1)

When Dreams Tremble by Radclyffe. Two women whose lives turned out far differently than they'd once imagined discover that sometimes the shape of the future can only be found in the past. (1-933110-64-3)

The Devil Unleashed by Ali Vali. As the heat of violence rises, so does the passion. A Casey Family crime saga. (1-933110-61-9)

Burning Dreams by Susan Smith. The chronicle of the challenges faced by a young drag king and an older woman who share a love "outside the bounds." (1-933110-62-7)

Fresh Tracks by Georgia Beers. Seven women, seven days. A lot can happen when old friends, lovers, and a new girl in town get together in the mountains. (1-933110-63-5)

The Empress and the Acolyte by Jane Fletcher. Jemeryl and Tevi fight to protect the very fabric of their world: time. Lyremouth Chronicles Book Three. (1-933110-60-0)

First Instinct by JLee Meyer. When high-stakes security fraud leads to murder, one woman flees for her life while another risks her heart to protect her. (1-933110-59-7)

Erotic Interludes 4: *Extreme Passions* ed. by Radclyffe and Stacia Seaman. Thirty of today's hottest erotica writers set the pages aflame with love, lust, and steamy liaisons. (1-933110-58-9)

Storms of Change by Radclyffe. In the continuing saga of the Provincetown Tales, duty and love are at odds as Reese and Tory face their greatest challenge. (1-933110-57-0)

Unexpected Ties by Gina L. Dartt. With death before dessert, Kate Shannon and Nikki Harris are swept up in another tale of danger and romance. (1-933110-56-2)

Sleep of Reason by Rose Beecham. While Detective Jude Devine searches for a lost boy, her rocky relationship with Dr. Mercy Westmoreland gets a lot harder. (1-933110-53-8)

Passion's Bright Fury by Radclyffe. Passion strikes without warning when a trauma surgeon and a filmmaker become reluctant allies. (1-933110-54-6)

Broken Wings by L-J Baker. When Rye Woods meets beautiful dryad Flora Withe, her libido, as hidden as her wings, reawakens along with her heart. (1-933110-55-4)

Combust the Sun by Andrews & Austin. A Richfield and Rivers mystery set in L.A. Murder among the stars. (1-933110-52-X)

Of Drag Kings and the Wheel of Fate by Susan Smith. A blind date in a drag club leads to an unlikely romance. (1-933110-51-1)

Tristaine Rises: Tristaine Book Three by Cate Culpepper. Brenna, Jesstin, and the Amazons of Tristaine face their greatest challenge for survival. (1-933110-50-3)

Too Close to Touch by Georgia Beers. Kylie O'Brien believes in true love and is willing to wait for it, even though Gretchen, her new boss, is off-limits. (1-933110-47-3)

100th Generation by Justine Saracen. Ancient curses, modern-day villains, and an intriguing woman lead archeologist Valerie Foret on the adventure of her life. (1-933110-48-1)

Battle for Tristaine: Tristaine Book Two by Cate Culpepper. While Brenna struggles to find her place in the clan, Tristaine is threatened with destruction. Second in the Tristaine series. (1-933110-49-X)

The Traitor and the Chalice by Jane Fletcher. Tevi and Jemeryl risk all in the race to uncover a traitor. The Lyremouth Chronicles Book Two. (1-933110-43-0)

Promising Hearts by Radclyffe. Dr. Vance Phelps arrives in New Hope, Montana, with no hope of happiness—until she meets Mae. (1-933110-44-9)

Carly's Sound by Ali Vali. Poppy Valente and Julia Johnson form a bond of friendship that becomes something far more. A poignant romance about love and renewal. (1-933110-45-7)

Unexpected Sparks by Gina L. Dartt. Kate Shannon's attraction to much younger Nikki Harris is complication enough without a fatal fire that Kate can't ignore. (1-933110-46-5)

Whitewater Rendezvous by Kim Baldwin. Two women on a wilderness kayak adventure discover that true love may be nothing at all like they imagined. (1-933110-38-4)

Erotic Interludes 3: *Lessons in Love* ed. by Radclyffe and Stacia Seaman. Sign on for a class in love…the best lesbian erotica writers take us to "school." (1-9331100-39-2)

Punk Like Me by JD Glass. Twenty-one-year-old Nina has a way with the girls, and she doesn't always play by the rules. (1-933110-40-6)

Coffee Sonata by Gun Brooke. Four women whose lives unexpectedly intersect in a small town by the sea share one thing in common—they all have secrets. (1-933110-41-4)

The Clinic: Tristaine Book One by Cate Culpepper. Brenna, a prison medic, finds herself drawn to Jesstin, a warrior reputed to be descended from ancient Amazons. (1-933110-42-2)

Forever Found by JLee Meyer. Can time, tragedy, and shattered trust destroy a love that seemed destined? Chance reunites childhood friends separated by tragedy. (1-933110-37-6)

Sword of the Guardian by Merry Shannon. Princess Shasta's bold new bodyguard has a secret that could change both of their lives. *He* is actually a *she*. (1-933110-36-8)

Wild Abandon by Ronica Black. Dr. Chandler Brogan and Officer Sarah Monroe are drawn together by their common obsessions—sex, speed, and danger. (1-933110-35-X)

Turn Back Time by Radclyffe. Pearce Rifkin and Wynter Thompson have nothing in common but a shared passion for surgery—and unexpected attraction. (1-933110-34-1)

Chance by Grace Lennox. A sexy, funny, touching story of two women who, in finding themselves, also find one another. (1-933110-31-7)

The Exile and the Sorcerer by Jane Fletcher. First in the Lyremouth Chronicles. Tevi and a shy young sorcerer face monsters, magic, and the challenge of loving. (1-933110-32-5)

A Matter of Trust by Radclyffe. When what should be just business turns into much more, two women struggle to trust the unexpected. (1-933110-33-3)

Sweet Creek by Lee Lynch. A celebration of the enduring nature of love, friendship, and community in the heart-warming lesbian community of Waterfall Falls. (1-933110-29-5)

The Devil Inside by Ali Vali. The head of a New Orleans crime organization falls for a woman who turns her world upside down. (1-933110-30-9)

Grave Silence by Rose Beecham. Detective Jude Devine's investigation of ritual murders is complicated by her torrid affair with pathologist Dr. Mercy Westmoreland. (1-933110-25-2)

Honor Reclaimed by Radclyffe. Secret Service Agent Cameron Roberts and Blair Powell close ranks to find the would-be assassins who nearly claimed Blair's life. (1-933110-18-X)

Honor Bound by Radclyffe. Secret Service Agent Cameron Roberts and Blair Powell face political intrigue, a clandestine threat to Blair's safety, and the seemingly irreconcilable differences that force them ever farther apart. (1-933110-20-1)

Innocent Hearts by Radclyffe. In a wild and unforgiving land, two women learn about love, passion, and the wonders of the heart. (1-933110-21-X)

The Temple at Landfall by Jane Fletcher. An imprinter, one of Celaeno's most revered servants of the Goddess, is also a prisoner to the faith—until a Ranger frees her by claiming her heart. The Celaeno series. (1-933110-27-9)

Protector of the Realm, Supreme Constellations Book One by Gun Brooke. A space adventure filled with suspense and a daring intergalactic romance. (1-933110-26-0)

Force of Nature by Kim Baldwin. From tornados to forest fires, the forces of nature conspire to bring Gable McCoy and Erin Richards close to danger, and closer to each other. (1-933110-23-6)

In Too Deep by Ronica Black. Undercover homicide cop Erin McKenzie tracks a femme fatale who just might be a real killer...with love and danger hot on her heels. (1-933110-17-1)

Erotic Interludes 2: *Stolen Moments* ed. by Radclyffe and Stacia Seaman. Love on the run, in the office, in the shadows...Fast, furious, and almost too hot to handle. (1-933110-16-3)

Course of Action by Gun Brooke. Actress Carolyn Black desperately wants the starring role in an upcoming film produced by Annelie Peterson. Just how far will she go for the dream part of a lifetime? (1-933110-22-8)

Rangers at Roadsend by Jane Fletcher. Sergeant Chip Coppelli has learned to spot trouble coming, and that is exactly what she sees in her new recruit, Katryn Nagata. The Celaeno series. (1-933110-28-7)

Justice Served by Radclyffe. Lieutenant Rebecca Frye and her lover, Dr. Catherine Rawlings, embark on a deadly game of hide-and-seek with an underworld kingpin who traffics in human souls. (1-933110-15-5)

Distant Shores, Silent Thunder by Radclyffe. Dr. Tory King—along with the women who love her—is forced to examine the boundaries of love, friendship, and the ties that transcend time. (1-933110-08-2)

Hunter's Pursuit by Kim Baldwin. A raging blizzard, a mountain hideaway, and a killer-for-hire set a scene for disaster—or desire—when Katarzyna Demetrious rescues a beautiful stranger. (1-933110-09-0)

The Walls of Westernfort by Jane Fletcher. All Temple Guard Natasha Ionadis wants is to serve the Goddess—until she falls in love with one of the rebels she is sworn to destroy. The Celaeno series. (1-933110-24-4)

Erotic Interludes: *Change Of Pace* by Radclyffe. Twenty-five hot-wired encounters guaranteed to spark more than just your imagination. Erotica as you've always dreamed of it. (1-933110-07-4)

Honor Guards by Radclyffe. In a wild flight for their lives, the president's daughter and those who are sworn to protect her wage a desperate struggle for survival. (1-933110-01-5)

Fated Love by Radclyffe. Amidst the chaos and drama of a busy emergency room, two women must contend not only with the fragile nature of life, but also with the irresistible forces of fate. (1-933110-05-8)

Justice in the Shadows by Radclyffe. In a shadow world of secrets and lies, Detective Sergeant Rebecca Frye and her lover, Dr. Catherine Rawlings, join forces in the elusive search for justice. (1-933110-03-1)